Daughters of Hui

Daughters of Hui

Xu Xi

(Sussy Chakó)

Asia 2000 Limited
Hong Kong

ISBN 962-7160-40-7

Published by Asia 2000 Ltd
1101 Seabird House,
22–28 Wyndham Street, Central,
Hong Kong

Typeset with Ventura Publisher in Adobe Garamond by Asia 2000
Printed in Hong Kong by Regal Printing

First printing 1996

For Tamas Aczel, in remembrance, of guns and complications . . .
and for Mike Morrow, a quiet American, and the squamous mind.

Moreover, acknowledgements, in lines of fine type. . . .

Thanks to Kingsley Bolton, and his persuasive powers at the Hong Kong U Library, a fine establishment; and to Kirpal Singh, for the truth in lies on a Singapore summer's night.

Contents

Your name or your person,
Which is dearer?

Tao Te Ching, Lao Tzu
Chapter XLIV, Book Two
(translated by D.C. Lau)

Danny's Snake

I

The Monday afternoon Rosemary picked up Danny hitch-hiking, his van had a flat tire. A snake coiled around his neck.

"Is it poisonous?" she asked.

"No, but it'll squeeze you to death if you let him."

She had recognized her former student, a tall pale figure, standing along Route 9 midway between Amherst and North-ampton. Leyland, she remembered, as she slowed down for him. Halfway down last semester's roll call computer printout — a Hampshire College student.

But a thirteen-foot boa! In her eight-year-old Toyota Celica. What would Manky say?

As she drove, reports of Tiananmen dominated the news. She could feel him watching her as they listened to the radio.

"Rosemary Hui." He let her name rest on his tongue, as if luxuriating in its shape and sound. "You're Chinese, aren't you?" His voice was deep, almost a bass.

"Yes," she replied.

"I hope you have no relatives in China."

"No. Only in Hong Kong," she said.

He did not raise the subject again, much to her relief. Since the start of Tiananmen she had found events in China too painful to discuss. Everyone she knew, all her friends, colleagues and even her students, seemed to expect her to have a lot to say about it. It was not a subject about which she trusted herself to speak.

They stopped at a light. Rosemary felt the summer sun warm her elbow, propped on the window edge. From the corner of her eye, she peered at the snake, which hung in a double loop around her passenger. Why wasn't she afraid of it, she wondered. Was it because its handler appeared calm, making the danger safe?

The news reported that a still unknown number of students were dead or seriously injured. She switched off the radio, and tried to quickly brush away a starting tear, hoping Danny wouldn't notice.

"I was going to go to China," he said. "To Tibet." He gazed out the window as he spoke.

That surprisingly deep voice again. Too rich and sensual for such a boy. Rosemary recalled his apologetic face the day he sat in her office last semester and said he was dropping her course. And how she had tried to tell him it was okay. She heard the same apology in his tone now. "You still can," she responded.

"Perhaps." He was silent a moment. And then, "I think my snake likes you."

She kept her eyes on the road. "Why so?"

"It's trying to say hi."

She glanced at her passenger. The snake had unwound itself from around him and was slithering towards her. Its head was almost at her shoulder. She drew back, startled by the proximity of this sleek reptile, imagining, for just a second, that she could feel its breath on her cheek. Danny yanked its head away, and placed it against his shoulder.

"I'm sorry," he said. "I didn't mean to scare you."

"That's okay. I wasn't really scared." But she felt a knot tighten in her stomach as she said this.

Danny had shifted and was leaning against the car door. The snake had circled its way around him, and its tail was an inch away from the gear stick. She glanced at him. *Leeang jai,* a beautiful boy, although she hadn't thought so before. There was an angular precision to his New England features. These were softened by the grace of his movements. He could be a dancer, the way his body seemed to flow into the too small passenger seat. She saw him dart out his right leg, winding his ankle in a swift, neat movement around the snake's tail to draw it away from the stick shift. He gazed steadily at her as he did this. Rosemary found herself blushing under his scrutiny.

They did not speak again the rest of the way.

She dropped him at the Sunoco off Route 9 near Haydenville. "Thanks," he said as he closed the door. "Hope I see you again."

She watched the snake slither down his body as he walked away. Her skin reacted, not with goose bumps, but of something much lighter, less prickly, smoothly dry. She wondered if he knew the effect he had had on her, and thought that he probably did. Only the tiniest pang of guilt recalled Man-Kit, her Manky, who inspired such absolute fidelity.

Driving home to Springfield, she switched PBS back on and listened to the jazz program. Charlie Parker playing *How Deep is the Ocean* in his surprisingly languid yet sharply curving tones made her think of the snake. It took a little more than half an hour to arrive at her apartment complex.

Man-Kit was hunched over his computer terminal when she entered. Even when deeply absorbed in his work, he always managed to look neat. His broad and rather flat face was smooth and unlined; the only wrinkles that creased his features appeared around the edges of his eyes when he smiled. Rosemary still marveled at how tidily his straight hair fell into place just above his neck. From time to time he would toss his head back, brushing away a lock of hair that fell across his forehead with the back of his hand.

The same jazz program she had been listening to blared through their sound system. She went over to kiss him, and saw that he was in the middle of one of his top speed computer chess games.

"Hey, Rosa-M. So are you ready to kill the kids yet?" he asked, his eyes still glued to the screen. They spoke to each other mostly in English, with occasional Cantonese phrases mixed in. It was something they had done since they first met in Hong Kong. While his left hand manipulated the keyboard, his right hand hovered over a timer, which he struck with a rhythmic regularity.

"Almost," she said. The swiftness of his moves made her dizzy.
"No mail."
"Good. I'm sick of bills anyway. Any calls?"
He never took his eyes off the screen. "Nothing important."
"By the way, did you hear Bird just now?"
"Huh? Oh why, was he on? I guess I didn't."
"Okay. I'll go cook."

She smiled as she walked away. Funny, but once he would have been the one to ask if she'd heard Bird and been beside himself if she hadn't noticed. A warm, slightly maternal feeling overtook her. Manky, her Manky may have lost some of his youthful figure — ever since his thirtieth birthday he seemed to have become a little softer, rounder — but he was still the only man who commanded her entire being, the only one who counted on her completely.

Rosemary put away her papers and books, and clipped up her long hair into a ponytail. From the kitchen she heard a slap on a table, and an exclamation of delight. Man-Kit had won yet another game. He appeared in the kitchen, jogged past her, circled back, spun her around away from the sink, and lifted all five feet of her off the ground. She pulled off his glasses, kissed him, and hopped out off his arms, giggling. He left her, then, to finish making dinner, grabbing a Coors Light from the fridge as he went out.

Later at dinner, she told him about Danny's snake.

"Was it edible?" he asked, at the end of her story.

Man-Kit loved snake soup, a delicacy Rosemary could have sooner done without, along with dog meat and monkey brains. She had spent her childhood up till age ten in Malaysia, on the island of Penang, her mother's birthplace, and felt that the infusion of Malay culture made her somehow less Chinese than him. But, as he often teasingly reminded her, she was one hundred percent pure blood Chinese, even if she was part Hokkienese from the lazy tropics.

"Well, I wouldn't cook it for you," she retorted, as she placed a plateful of fried noodles on the table.

"Look," he said, picking up several strands of noodles off the serving platter with his chopsticks and waving them in the air, "snake, snake!"

She gave him her school teacher look. Handing him the bottle of chili sauce, she sat down to dinner.

Man-Kit ate hungrily, quickly, the way he always did. He ate Cantonese style, the bowl close to his lips, shoveling food into his mouth with his chopsticks. Rosemary picked at the noodles. Cooking always made her feel full. Unlike her husband, she did not like to eat as soon as the food was ready. He insisted that dinner had to start when the food was piping hot straight from the wok, the steam still rising from it. She preferred to wait, allowing the aroma to build up her appetite.

But one thing they both agreed on was chili sauce. Rosemary had converted him to her love for spicy foods, and now, he used chili sauce the way Americans used ketchup — on everything.

They ate in silence.

After about his third mouthful, he said, "So tell me more about the snake man. Was he a charmer as well?"

He laughed at his own joke, and she made a face.

"Nothing to tell."

"Was he a good student? What grade did he get?"

"I."

"I?"

"Incomplete. He wanted it, even though I told him not to bother. My only one to date."

She could feel Man-Kit gnawing away inside her. The terrible thing about their closeness, their incessant togetherness, was that he controlled every square inch of privacy within her. She had liked the closeness at first, even insisted on it, while he had tried to distance himself. Now, after seven years, after he had given in to her insistence, she was beginning to feel slightly claustrophobic.

"You know," she said, "I think maybe I should consider a new dissertation thesis."

"Why, what's changing your mind?"

"Oh, I'm not really sure. Maybe I don't really want a PhD after all."

Man-Kit did not respond.

She let a reasonable interval lapse before saying, "So what do you think?"

"It's a crisis. What do you want me to say?"

"Well surely you have something to say about this. It's not everyday that I might consider making such a big change."

"Is that why you picked up a hitchhiker? So you wouldn't have to think about what you really want to do, like you're supposed to do while driving?"

It was an old joke. Their moving to Springfield meant a commute to the university at Amherst for her. She had insisted on moving, so that his commute to work would be easier since he hated to drive. Her promise had been that the drive would be crisis-solving time.

"Eat," she said, pretending not to smile. But she felt the familiar rush of pleasure that assailed her each time she was reminded how truly well he knew her.

Later, in bed, while he fiddled with the alarm clock, she stretched herself across his back and nibbled his ear.

"Make love to me, Manky," she whispered.

He removed her gently, and rolled over on his back. He was silent for a moment. "Listen," he said, "I have to go home."

His declaration made her sit up. It took a minute to sink in.

"Your father?"

He nodded. "He's really bad."

"But when did you find out?"

"Mom called this morning, just after you left for class."

She heard the pain and fear in his voice. Over the last year, they had heard from his mother as often as once a month about his father's worsening condition. And each time, he had dismissed the reality by their distance. Neither of them had been back to Hong Kong nor seen their families in the six years since their arrival in the States. That was mostly her choice, she knew.

And now, she knew he did not expect her to go.

Despite herself, she sensed the usual jealousy creeping in. She fought the feeling, forcing herself to empathize. "You have to go, don't you?"

"I spoke to Ah Chun in New York. There's a flight on Thursday, but on such short notice, it's nine hundred. . . ."

She interrupted him. "It doesn't matter," she said, cradling his head in her arms, "the money doesn't matter."

She had to say it because she knew he couldn't. Most of her life, unlike for Manky, money had simply been there. But, even as she said it, she knew that this meant yet another extension of their already over-extended credit cards. For the first time, the thought frightened her.

Rosemary switched off the light. They curled into each other.

"I don't know if I can face it alone," he whispered again.

She felt his body shaking, ever so slightly, as he drifted off to sleep in her arms.

Her poor, wounded hero — how could he have held that back all day long? Three years ago, she would have reacted with much more annoyance and surprise, questioning him insistently, wanting to know why he hadn't said something sooner, why he didn't trust her enough to ask her help and how he could keep this from her. And he would have retreated further into himself until finally, when he couldn't hold back his temper anymore, he would shout at her to leave him alone and she would retort that he didn't need to yell and they would both eventually fall back, she in tears and he in a funk that would last at least another forty-eight hours, if not longer.

Well, at least they were past most of that, and now she could let him sleep, although she knew he would wrestle all night with his dreams. Man-Kit never slept peacefully. He always held everything deep inside himself and let his sleep bear the brunt. In their four years of marriage, she had been awakened many nights by his grinding teeth, flailing arms and kicking legs. Yet when she complained, he laughed and said he was just practising *kung fu.*

Rosemary heard his even breathing. Lying on her back, she closed her eyes and tried, unsuccessfully, to fall asleep. She lay awake for almost an hour. She wished they could have made love. Why did the refuge of their love have to be so fragile and uncertain? Why didn't Man-Kit trust her enough to ask for help? Yet a nagging voice inside told her she shouldn't be blaming Manky. What she hadn't said to him, had trouble saying even to herself, was that she did not want him to go away from her. And this she knew he understood.

II

She drove back alone to Springfield from Kennedy Airport. The flight for Hong Kong had actually been on time at noon, much to her dismay. She had hoped for more time with Man-Kit. Before she knew it, he was kissing her, kissing her so much that her whole being ached. Then he was running towards customs. "I'll call you," he cried.

They hadn't even had time to stop for a meal in Chinatown.

Her only consolation was that they had made love early that morning, and Man-Kit had been as crazily passionate as she knew he could be.

To distract herself, she turned on the radio. More reports of events in China. At the Chinese students' demonstration in Amherst the other day, she had donated, almost without thinking, some fifty dollars to their cause. She had simply looked silently at Man-Kit as she took the money out of her purse. For once, he had not teased her about what he called her lovingly lavish bleeding heart.

On the night they had watched the television reports of the lone student in his futile joust with the tanks, Man-Kit had comforted her while she wept and whispered, "Why now, why us?"

How completely he understood.

Suddenly the thought struck her: was it possible that Man-Kit, her Manky, might be gone for a long time?

Their last three days had been a race of frenzied phone calls, organizing and planning. There hadn't been time for her to stop and really consider that in the seven years since they first met they had never been apart for more than even a couple of days.

Despite the anxiety she felt, the realization made her smile.

Seven years ago, she and a group of friends had walked into Rick's Café in Tsimshatsui after a dance at the University. Her Shakespeare professor had directed their group there for the must-hear experience of live jazz. Her Shakespeare professor was a horny young South African who would do anything to get close to her in a dark place now that she had graduated and could no longer compromise his position.

But her mind was not on him at all. For the first time ever, she was going to see and hear live jazz in Hong Kong!

It had been quite a novelty. She had listened, not fully comprehending the sounds she heard, trying to piece them into her memory of a late night radio program she sometimes listened to on the English language station hosted by a Portuguese deejay, Tony da Costa, who had already initiated her to the strange jazz albums he brought back from the US.

Manky was on the bandstand, drumming away. He was lean and energetic, his lips set in a determined line as he handled the rhythm for the all-Caucasian band. Man-Kit, during the break, strolled casually by her group to say hello to someone he knew. And the next thing she knew, Shakespeare was edged aside while Ho Man-Kit glided into position next to her, his arm neatly barring the South African's progress.

"Didn't anyone tell you Hong Kong girls don't like jazz?" he asked, and somehow kept her laughing and talking for the rest of the night. And before she knew it she was agreeing to see him the very next night. Why had he ever let go of that jazz life?

A siren wail recalled her rudely to the present.

Rosemary pulled over.

"You know you were doing at least seventy?" the officer said, as he wrote up her ticket.

"Sorry about that."

"Hey, didn't I give you a ticket a couple of weeks ago?"

No, she wanted to say, we all look alike. If Manky had been home, she would have done so. But she held her tongue and smiled politely, knowing that the officer was right about the previous ticket.

Stupid laws, she thought, when he finally returned her license. Guiltily, she thought of Man-Kit, who no longer chided her about her many tickets, and who never himself speeded, except at his computer. But the waste of money, she knew, bothered him, although he was used to her extravagances. Perhaps she would never be as worried about money as he was, but a tug of conscience had recently begun to assail her, which she found stifling and irritating. He never said so, but sometimes she thought he had stopped playing drums because jazz simply didn't pay, and computers did. She drove at fifty-five the rest of the way, and stopped daydreaming.

She arrived home to find a van parked in front of her house, and Danny at her door with a bouquet of orchids. He stared at her as she approached. "I guess dreams come true." He spoke softly, almost in an undertone.

Rosemary looked at the tan uniform he was wearing with SPRINGFIELD FLORISTS stitched on the pocket, trying not to react to the timbre of his voice.

Danny cradled the flowers in his left arm. "These are for Mrs. Ho. Do you know her?"

"That's me."

"But . . . I thought you were Rosemary Hui?"

His obvious disappointment pleased her. "Hui's my maiden name. I use it at school."

He continued to gaze as if overwhelmed by her presence. And then, recovering his composure, "Here, I guess someone had these delivered to you."

She fumbled for her keys, and dropped them. When she stooped to pick them up, she almost lost her balance and was steadied by Danny's hand. It disturbed her to be so clumsy.

"Why don't you come in for a moment?" she offered.

He entered.

She opened the card from Man-Kit which said *I already miss you Rosa-M, Manky.* It made her want to cry.

"I hope they're happy flowers."

"Sort of."

She cried a little anyway, in between smiles and frowns, thinking that despite their modest means, his extravagances were always far more worthwhile than hers. She kept her face turned away as she arranged the orchids in a vase. Gorgeous white, mauve and tiger striped orchids, just like the ones that grew wild in the Malaysian countryside. All the time, Danny stood by the door.

Sentimental fool, she scolded herself. Drying her eyes, she turned back to him, smiling.

"Beautiful flowers, don't you think?" she asked.

"Yes," he paused, "but not so happy."

"No."

It had slipped out, that "no", to this virtual stranger. Yet he seemed gentle, she thought, and kind.

"Please," she said, "I don't mean to keep you from your job."

"That's okay. You're my last delivery today. Besides, I've still got that 'incomplete' on my transcript."

She smiled. "Since I hadn't heard from you, I assumed you were going to let it turn into a W."

"W?"

"Withdrawal."

Danny was gazing at her again. His large, rather beautiful green eyes and long lashes had a disarmingly innocent quality that made Rosemary blush, and she averted her face so that he wouldn't notice. She was embarrassed by the effect he had on her.

"You look like someone I know," he said, abruptly.

"Who?"

"An-Mei, my Mandarin tutor."

"We all look alike," she said, finally dispelling the traffic cop.

But he was undaunted, and continued to talk about An-Mei, "peace and beauty". He stayed until just before dinner time, talking, telling her all about himself. Boy's stuff, Manky would have called it. He was from Malden, near Boston. Delivering flowers and photographing reptiles for nature magazines earned him a living. College just wasn't his thing, not even at Hampshire's open curriculum, not even as an "older" student, which he was, being twenty-three. He studied Chinese up at UMASS, and wanted to go to China, to Tibet, he said. That would be his education, a life study, not just words in books. The unrest in China only made it all the more important for him to go. When he spoke, his words unwound with a sinuous intensity, as if he had waited forever for this moment of utterance.

Rosemary listened, surprised. Surprised that he spun Buddhist Tibet and Han China into the same mental tapestry. But students, she knew, suffered from knowledge gaps, pieces in the jigsaw that might take them years to find. It was just their enthusiasm and hurry to embrace all before they were ready. What surprised her more was how much he talked. He had not previously impressed her as the garrulous kind. In class, he had been the quiet American kid among mostly foreign students who fought to get into her section. She vaguely remembered the one paper he had submitted.

It had been short, little more than a page, and had been about Taoism. He used language well, but didn't really have much to say.

"Tibet must be incredible," he was saying.

"The Chinese don't like the Tibetans, you know," Rosemary interrupted his ecstasy.

"Don't they?" He seemed surprised. "Is Hong Kong much like China? You're from Hong Kong, right?"

She felt just a little sorry for him as he continued to talk. Perhaps he would have a wonderful experience in China. Somehow, she didn't think so. China might be a paper tiger, as Manky and their Hong Kong friends sometimes liked to say, but Rosemary believed the country devoured its young mercilessly. And Danny was young, was full of desire to conquer a world, any world, one which only he would define. He seemed like some of her ESL English-as-a-second-language students. They came to America on the strength of a dream, only to be disappointed, and who, until forced into a private conference away from the classroom, would not open up and speak freely.

It made sense when he told her he was a jazz musician. She had been around enough of them to know. It fitted with his musical voice, his overall fluidity, his odd alienation as an American who wasn't like the rest of his peers, but was still undeniably American.

On Sunday nights, he said, he jammed at a club in Springfield.

"During the last set, with Joel's band?" she asked.

His face perked up at her question. "Yes, how did you know?"

"My husband used to play drums many moons ago. I know the club you mean."

The memory of an earlier life nudged its way into her consciousness.

Danny invited her, then, to see him on Sunday.

"What's your axe?" she asked.

"Bari sax."

She imagined him on stage, his hands wrapped around the large, unwieldy instrument, which had such a rich, rarely-heard sound. At least he was tall enough. "Will your snake be there?"

He smiled. "In his cage."

After Danny left, she wandered around the apartment, trying to decide what to do next. It was almost seven. She should eat. Since a hurried breakfast in the morning, she hadn't eaten all day. Surely there was something she could tempt herself with?

But there was no Manky to cook for. Hungry, lovable Manky.

What a little housewife she had become! When Manky had still been in graduate school, he had done his share of the cooking. Since his graduation a year ago, however, she had taken over the preparation of all their meals, even though he protested, saying that as long as he had the time, why shouldn't he do his share? She had been adamant, insisting that since their future residence in America depended entirely on his ability to establish himself in the work world, she wanted him to be freed of daily chores.

If their friends back home could see her now, how they would laugh. She had always been the one who complained that Hong Kong life was too restrictive for a woman, and that she wouldn't have to behave in such an old fashioned way in America. Even when she and Manky had first arrived in the States, all she had willingly done was cook, which she found creative and fun, and had only done housework grudgingly. And Manky, dear Manky, had not minded in the least. He had taken over the maintenance of their household, his instinctive neatness abhorring the mess she left.

Her dissertation beckoned. Stubbornly, she ignored it.

Funny, she thought, how seven years in a new country could change her.

Now, she would happily be a housewife, Manky's wife, and give up everything she had worked for as long as he would always be there. Of course, they had both changed. It didn't seem so long ago that Manky was telling her the reason he wanted to go to UMASS had more to do with Max Roach's ongoing tenure there and programs like Jazz in July, than with the graduate school in computer science.

She made a small pot of coffee, ignoring all her Chinese teas sitting untouched over the years in their larder, and prepared a ham and cheese sandwich.

She did not touch her dissertation that night.

III

There was something about Danny, she told Man-Kit, when he called to say that he did not know how long he would have to stay in Hong Kong.

"Oh, oh," he said, "he'll fall in love with you while you fall in love with his snake."

Rosemary laughed. "He's much too young for me."

"Right. Like Americans don't still card you?"

Both in their early thirties, they could almost pass as college kids, although she teased Man-Kit that his expanding beer belly was the giveaway. They often joked about their youthful appearances, a joke they played on all Americans. It was a joke of which she was growing tired the longer she lived in the States. But she detected some antagonism in his tone — not jealousy, Man-Kit rarely expressed any jealousy — just the tiniest flicker of resentment that he could not be there to share the joke.

She knew that now was the moment to reassure him, to arouse him by telling him she needed him sexually. She could use what they called their ESL sex words. Then, any tension between them would subside, and he would whisper to her the few Malay words she had taught him, and she would reply in Cantonese or sometimes, Mandarin, their love words. *Lingua franca.*

But instead, she said. "He's playing Sunday at the Midnite Lite. He asked me to come."

There was a short, but deafening pause.

"Boys' games," he said, at last. "If you're really American."

"Which we'll never be." She could at least offer him that little bit of reassurance.

"Games are necessary."

She heard the spark in his voice, any antagonism gone. It was something he said often, something that always cheered her. She was glad he hadn't gotten really angry — Manky always got so unreasonably furious, followed by depression when he let his temper get the better of him. Why had she egged him on? To make him jealous? It wasn't something she generally did. But then, being this much apart wasn't something they ever did, and no reason was reason enough for this separation as far as she was concerned.

And then, he told her about the miles of demonstrators, how beautiful and terrible this outpouring was, previously so repressed. People from all walks of life marched into the streets to confront the inevitable change to the status quo, whatever the change would bring. Was it fear, she asked, and perhaps humiliation at their helplessness, their loss of control? No, he replied, people were angry and outraged, not afraid, more indignant than humiliated. It was a protest, a demand to be heard. It was unlike anything he had ever seen in Hong Kong.

"In the end, I'm glad we decided to stay in America," he said.

"Games and all?"

"And all." His tone was certain, without its usual ambivalence.

Before he hung up, he told her that he had run into Sonny Lee, an old friend from his rock-DJ days, who was now a popular local singer. He said Sonny's latest single was playing on all the Chinese-language radio stations. She thought she detected a note of wistfulness in his voice as he said this. He had drummed for Sonny for a brief time, but complained that the music was a poor sellout to commercial Western rock. Was he thinking now that he had sold out too?

Before she hung up, she told him in Cantonese that she was lying naked in bed, her long hair spread over the pillow, waiting for him. A ripple of pleasure prickled her as she spoke.

When Rosemary walked into the Midnite Lite on Sunday, she was pleased to find nothing had changed. The same iron door marked the entrance to the club, on a back alley in downtown Springfield. A former speakeasy of prohibition days, it legally held no more than forty people; only newcomers were asked to pay the cover charge. Man-Kit had played there for at least two years, and it was almost as long since he had played at all. His drum set, he was fond of saying, was his contribution to their as yet non-existent art collection.

The band was on break before the last set. Joel, the house sax player and club owner greeted her with a hug. His arm looped into hers as they chatted.

"And Manky? What's he up to these days?"

"Programming relational databases. Creating confluence for many meandering tributaries of bits and bytes. He's been working hard since he finished his master's."

"Always the hustler. Tell him we miss him around here. And you, gorgeous as ever, what are you doing these days? What brings you out tonight besides my musical talent and never-ending desire to seduce you?"

"Oh, nothing different. Still teaching foreign and American students how to write. Still waiting to have children."

She hadn't meant to say that about children. She and Man-Kit had agreed to wait until their life in America was more settled. The trouble was, she was beginning to feel slightly old, slightly tired of always having to wait for everything as if she didn't deserve what she wanted. Also, she knew that a grandchild, especially if it were a boy, was someone that her dad would embrace happily, even willingly, despite Man-Kit, the "undesirable" husband. Age seemed to soften her feelings towards her father, making her want the same things he wanted.

Seeing Danny, she disengaged her arm and indicated the cage he was carrying, glad for the opportunity to change the subject.

"The snake. I came to see the snake."

She saw Joel's eyebrows rise. "Oh, him eh? Didn't know you guys knew him. I should have known Man-Kit wouldn't leave you unattended while he disappeared to the other side of the world."

She heard the chuckle in his voice, but saw him eye Danny suspiciously. Same old Joel. Fat, fifty and twice divorced, he ran the Midnite Lite as a jazz club with a passion. Although he lambasted rock bands, and bemoaned the lack of serious, young jazz musicians, a new musician, no matter how talented, never won quick acceptance on his bandstand. And though he flirted out-rageously and often, he observed, and protected, the sanctity of other people's relationships with an almost pious reverence. Man-Kit called him the one-man jazz and morality DoD.

Danny approached them. Rosemary thought he looked uneasy, and guessed that he had not yet won Joel over.

"Sit in on the second tune, kid," said Joel. "Talk to you later, Rosa-M."

Joel left them.

"May I buy you a drink?" she offered.

They went to the bar together and he accepted a beer. He carried the cage and his saxophone case with him. The snake lay unmov-ing, entwined in a pile of brown and black scales, its tail sloped over its neck.

She gazed at the snake.

"It's one big muscle, you know," he said. "All muscle."

The house band straggled onto the stage.

"Does he always call you Rosa-M?"

She had not expected the question, had not thought, in fact, that he would have observed this small familiarity.

"Yes, he does. Everyone does."

They were standing at the bar facing each other. Out of the corner of her eye, she caught Joel watching them. Danny seemed oblivious to this surveillance.

"Rosemary. Remembrance. A much prettier name. I hoped you'd come."

His words sprang out suddenly after a measured pause. This was the man, not the boy, romancing her. She was flattered by his attention. He remained so still whenever he spoke, as if speaking were a painful act. Even at her house, when he had talked quite incessantly, he had done so with a minimum of gestures or movement. Yet there was a soothing, fluid quality in his voice which she found sensual. Almost unbearably so.

She glanced down at the snake, avoiding his eyes.

"I'm not making that up, you know. Rosemary really does stand for remembrance."

There was a confidence in the way he said it, in his whole manner tonight, without the boyish enthusiasm that prevailed when he tried to talk about China. He removed his instrument from his case, never taking his eyes off her. As he adjusted the strap round his neck, securing the mouth of the bari sax at the right level for his lips, he suddenly winked at her. It was unnerving. But the way he handled his axe, his whole demeanor, suggested a musician who knew the scene and had no qualms about his own ability to perform well.

The band had launched into *'Round Midnight,* signaling the start of the last set during which outsiders were welcome to sit in. When Joel bought the club ten years ago, he had kept this signature tune which had been adopted by the previous owner. Only the house band played it, never the musicians who came to jam.

The music gave her an excuse not to respond. She turned towards the stage and listened, her back half turned to Danny. From the corner of her eye, she saw him lick the reed mouthpiece in preparation, his eyes still on her. She imagined his eyes on her hair, on her back, and his tongue sliding over her neck. His attention was unbearably exciting.

As the tune ended, he leaned close to her ear and said, "You're very beautiful."

"Thank you," she replied, and immediately regretted her response. It had been too automatic, cutting him off. She had not meant to do that.

He set the cage next to her. "Watch my snake, please?"

She nodded, wondering why she felt no fear. Danny stepped towards the bandstand where Joel relinquished the stage to him.

Danny called *"How Deep is the Ocean."* His tone was rich and layered. Again, she was struck by his seeming wispiness as he coaxed sounds from his bari sax. Except for his surprisingly deep voice, she would have expected him to play alto. He looked too thin and insubstantial to evoke such sensuality.

He played the way he spoke, with a minimum of bodily movement. His notes were varied and plentiful. And then, Rosemary recognized what he was doing. He had taken Bird's version, the same Parker tune she had heard just the other day with Al Haig on piano and Max Roach on drums, and transcribed and transposed it for his axe.

Joel joined her at the bar.

"The kid's got talent, I hate to admit," he said at the end of the tune, "even if he is a little too uptight."

"He's just young," she said. "You know, he hasn't had time to shape his sound."

"Aah, he's all over the place. Kids. Never know when it's time to come back to earth."

There was a pause. "You don't like him, do you?" It was less of a question than a statement.

"Do you?"

He spared her a reply by walking away as Danny returned.

She called Man-Kit when she got home that night. He was depressed, and she cheered him by sending greetings from Joel and the rest of the band. He was glad to hear that she had gone to the Midnite Lite. Somehow, the sensuality Danny evoked, which had occupied all her thoughts on the way home, waned the minute she heard Man-Kit's voice.

"And your father?" She wanted to know.

"Bad."

Man-Kit continued. "But not so bad that he couldn't ask if I was still making loud Western noises on the drums."

"And what did he say when you told him about your computer work?"

"*Din lo* — electronic brain — is just a Western abacus, and that I was selling out. As if his colonial idolatry weren't worse!"

Man-Kit had only been gone five days. His absence bothered her terribly, and already seemed much longer. Yet her unease at their separation felt natural and inevitable. They had often been told that they spent an unusual amount of time together for a married couple. But then, people didn't understand.

"So how long, Manky?"

"I just don't know. It could be as much as a month, maybe more."

She was glad she could not see his expression, an expression, she was sure, of resignation and complacency. When it came to family, Man-Kit accepted way too much. It irritated her.

"But what is it? What do the doctors say?"

"It's not that. Dad's just old and he wants me to be here to talk to. You know, like what I'm supposed to do for Mom and all that. He keeps saying that a Chinese son shouldn't be too far away from his father."

"What about your job, and me? Don't your family have anything to say about that? Don't they know you could jeopardize your visa status?"

"They don't understand, Rosa-M. Be fair. They've not been to America. How would they know how things are for us?"

But she knew he would not say to them how much he depended on her, nor that money was tight. It was so important for him to appear successful to them.

She pictured him at "home," in his family's apartment on the nineteenth floor of a building on a hillside of Hong Kong Island. His father was a retired Hong Kong government official who had wanted him to study in England and return to Hong Kong. His mother and two sisters lived what he termed a petty bourgeois existence. Man-Kit was the eldest child and only son.

"You can't stay that long. Surely they don't expect you to."

She heard the sigh of exasperation in his voice.

Shortly after they first met, he had told her, "You wouldn't like it at my home. My sisters go to the hairdresser's every week. My mother plays *mahjeuk* and talks about how little money she has, especially in relation to her friends. And Dad bad-mouths America, even though he's never even been there."

"My father's ill, Rosa-M. He might die." He paused. "They're my family. Please don't be unreasonable."

She had soon discovered that, despite his complaints, he was really fond of his family. And she knew she was being unreasonable. She tried to soften her tone. "Don't be impatient. I just miss you, that's all. You're my family now."

When he did not respond, she knew what he was thinking. "Did you speak to my father?" she asked.

"I went to see him. He was kind about my father. You know, he really does care about you. He offered us plane tickets for you to come and visit."

Her own eagerness startled her. "Did he really?"

"Yes he did."

There was a moment's silence during which Rosemary imagined going home to her dad, and apologizing in person for the rift that had separated them.

Manky continued, "You know, he's thinking of remarrying."

She did not know, of course, and the hesitation in Manky's voice made her brace. "She's young, isn't she?"

Manky didn't reply.

"How old?"

"Twenty-five."

So much for the eagerness. "Just young enough to be my little sister. Is she a hooker?"

"Come on, Rosa-M, give your father some credit."

And then, all the contempt she had ever felt for her father returned, and all she wanted was for Manky, her Manky, to be back in her arms, to be the only family she would ever want or need.

"I miss you," she whispered, crying softly. "It's too lonely without you."

"Please don't cry. This won't go on forever."

"I feel so foolish," she said, drying her eyes. "I shouldn't need you so much."

"It's the same for me too," he said.

He told her then that he would come home as soon as possible. She could tell he was unhappy with her.

It was almost one a.m. when she finally let him off. The Man-Kit she pictured putting down the phone half a world away was quite different from the image he had presented seven years ago. Her flashy, independent, temperamental jazz musician was really a family man. She remembered, only too clearly, how bitterly he had complained that his family didn't understand him. *Chi sin,* crazy, they called him. One of his sisters had laughingly told her that Man-Kit was even crazy as a baby; he had howled whenever anyone tried to rock him. His retort was that none of his family had enough rhythm to rock him.

But this was their family's way of loving and accepting each other, and she knew she resented it.

Rosemary switched off the lights in the living room, shut all the blinds and headed towards the bedroom. How desolate their apartment felt. The news about her father angered her. It was typical. Years of screwing prostitutes after her mother died — Rosemary had been twelve at the time but had quickly, too quickly, comprehended — and now, he was finally going to marry someone who was virtually one.

She remembered, seven years ago, when she first came home with the news that she was applying for an assistantship to study in America. How unsettled her father had been! Her university education, he said, was just the modern way for girls to pass the time before marriage. His idea was that she should marry the son of his business partner, and become a Hong Kong society lady who sat around sipping afternoon tea at the Mandarin. She thought he secretly blamed Man-Kit, who encouraged her endeavors. But if her father were angry at her, he failed to show it, choosing instead a perpetual silence about the subject once she had made her decision and left home. And she responded to his reticence by a stubborn refusal to take any money from him once she went to live with Manky, and none since she arrived in the States. For a long time, their communication had been almost non-existent. Certainly, she had never bothered to go home to visit.

"Apologize?" she had almost shouted at Manky when he first suggested her doing so three years ago. "Why should I apologize to him?"

Manky had remained unusually level-headed. "Because he's your father, and because one day he'll be gone before you've reconciled with him."

It had been the year of her father's sixtieth birthday, the age Confucius prescribed for "attuning one's ear to the decrees of the heavens". It would be a sad year for him, Manky said, if father and child still remained at odds, especially at a time when he was surely feeling his mortality.

"But why should I be the one? Why can't he come to me and say he was wrong, as he must know now. He can't always be right."

"This is not about right and wrong. It's a simple, filial matter — you're the daughter, he's the father. End of story. Come on, I don't have to tell you that."

All year long Manky had patiently, persistently tried to persuade her. In the end, she had given in, on the eve of her father's birthday. And she had called to apologize, an apology he accepted readily, saying they need never speak of their rift again. She remembered the warmth in her father's voice, a warmth she had seldom felt. Now, she and her father were at least on tentative speaking terms.

"I'll always be there to take care of you," Manky had said tonight on the phone, just before he hung up. "Don't cry, don't worry anymore. I'll be back and everything will be like it was, better even."

She went into the bathroom and began brushing her teeth. If only she could be angry! She knew she was stretching Manky; her unreasonableness and jealousy signaled to him that she blamed his family for taking him away from her. Anger would be easier to bear than this hollowness, this loneliness in the face of death. Yet what else could he do? This was family. He might be their only male relative soon. She understood his duty. She was Chinese too. But not *that* Chinese. She wouldn't know where to stand in the funeral procession if she were there, or be able to mourn.

If only she could really understand this feeling of family for someone other than Manky. But she had never properly accepted her husband's family, and now, could not go back to her own. Yet this Chinese way, Confucius' legacy, was rooted so deeply in them both. It felt all wrong and desperately unfair.

She continued brushing her teeth for almost seven minutes, until the foam covered her mouth. When she gargled, she saw she had made her gums bleed.

IV

A week later, she saw Danny again.

He appeared at her office, just at the end of her hours. Neither of her two office mates were there. It was almost five, and the early evening sun streamed through the window, casting the entire room in a dusky, surreal glare.

"Hello Rosemary." He lingered over her name. "I came to do something about that 'incomplete'."

He leaned against the door, his right hip bracing his person. His arm was raised above his head, the fingers resting above the door frame.

"Come in and sit." She watched his movements, flowing and graceful, as he slid into the chair by her desk. He was in cutoffs and a T-shirt. His long bare legs stretched out, his sandaled feet almost touched hers.

Rosemary was suddenly conscious of her thin summer dress, and her bare arms and legs. Danny's eyes smiled at her.

"You don't have to do anything about it, you know," she said.

"I want to."

"But why? You know you don't need a writing course."

"I think I can learn something from you."

She felt her age as she looked at him. Her eyes took in his physique, and it both excited and disturbed her. She tried to focus on what he was saying.

"Danny, what is it you think you want?"

"Truthfully?"

Rosemary hesitated. She knew where this was going, but gave in. "Of course, truthfully. And I'll take it with as many grains of salt as I choose."

"I just want to be around you."

She smiled, sure of herself now. "You don't need to write me papers to do that."

He reddened, and she caught herself thinking how sweet and vulnerable he looked. Rosemary leaned forward slightly, and crossed her legs. She watched his eyes follow her every motion.

Danny stared at her, saying nothing for nearly a minute. And then, he said, "I'm sorry. I'm being rude. I don't mean to stare."

The deep, sensual quality in his voice had returned.

"Rosemary, please come photograph my snake with me. It's only a slightly illegal endeavor, keeping a thirteen-foot snake, I mean. You know, a cop once stopped me and said I couldn't keep a snake over nine feet long, so I offered it to him to take away. He refused."

"It's not the illegality that's the problem," she said, smiling.

"I just want some company, that's all."

She had no more papers to grade. There was no Manky to bug her into working on her dissertation. Why shouldn't she?

"Yes, perhaps I will," she replied.

She followed his van for about three miles along 116 until they reached a clearing. Games, that was all this was. Just games. Just like the time Manky had been pursued by the Vietnamese girl who wanted "to be a jazz singer more than anything else in life" until she discovered he was married. And Manky had led her on, knowing full well she was more enamored of him than of jazz, promising to help her with her singing. How jealous Rosemary remembered she had been! And how Manky loved to tease her about it.

Danny's Snake

Danny parked, took out the cage, knelt down and set it on the roadside. His tall, lanky body curved gracefully as he worked. How unlike Manky he was, she thought as she watched him. Manky, despite his nimble mind, was a klutz except when seated at his drums or computer.

He unlatched the cage and released the snake.

The creature stretched out its entire length on the sandy roadside. Danny had placed it a foot away from her.

"One long muscle," he said. "Digesting, breathing, sensing danger. Did you know snakes won't attack unless you frighten them, and then they retaliate? I've had it since it was a baby, yet to it, I'm no different than the next guy. It could turn on me if I accidentally frightened it."

He held up his camera and began to shoot.

The early evening June sun was warm. Rosemary's gaze never left the snake as it inched forward, going nowhere in particular. It looked remarkably harmless lying there on the ground.

"Snakes like the sun," he continued. "They're timid creatures, kind of repressed, you know. All they really want to do is lie around basking in the sun all day. It's not a bad life being a snake."

Rosemary leaned against his car, her memory stirred by the sight of Danny's snake. In the Penang snake temple, when she'd been a girl, she had seen big snakes like boas and pythons in cages. But the little green vipers roamed around freely, dazed by the incense. Once, she had gone to the temple with her mother and some cousins. Her mother had leaned too hard against a gate, dislodging a viper curled around the top, and screamed as the snake fell on her shoulder.

"Is all your family in Hong Kong?"

"Just my father. My mother's dead."

"Were you close to her?"

"She always made me feel safe." Rosemary paused, the memories taking over. It was strange, talking about her mother to him. She seldom spoke about her, even to Manky; the loss was still too difficult to bear.

"You know," she continued, almost to herself, "she told me once that I would always be safe if I took my fears and made up silly reasons for them to go away. I was pretty timid as a child, scared of the dark, of the oily man — he was a kind of Malaysian bogey man — even of having to grow up. When I told her I wanted to be her little girl forever, she laughed and said my daddy wouldn't let me. I asked her why not and she said because then, he couldn't grow old and everyone has to grow old, but if she promised not to grow old would I stop being afraid? I didn't know what she meant, but somehow, that made me feel better, and I promised her. Silly reasons are better than no reasons, I guess, even if they make sense only in their own crazy way."

Danny was watching her closely.

"I'm rambling," she said, embarrassed.

"No," he said, "just remembering." He aimed his camera at her. "Smile."

She complied, grateful to break the strange mood brought on by remembrances.

"When did you start playing jazz?" she asked, as he snapped her.

"I don't know. Since I was about thirteen I think. My sister taught me, on the piano, and I spent a year listening to everything I could. Later, when I was about sixteen, I started hanging out in Boston with the students from Berklee. You know, the jazz school? This guy turned me onto Pepper Adams and bari sax, and I've been playing ever since. Yeah I know, I'm pretty good."

It was less of a boast than a statement of fact.

"But why this whole China thing? Why not music?"

He shrugged. "Who knows? I love the music, but it doesn't own me."

He spoke with such certainty, such finality, it seemed. Rosemary felt there was no leeway to probe further.

After he finished shooting and had put the snake back in its cage, he asked her, "So where's your husband?"

She explained.

"Then," he said, "I'll bring you flowers every day. Dozens of orchids to throw at your feet, like the royalty of Thailand."

"And what would you want in return?" She said this playfully, trying to be lighthearted. But she felt him encircling her with his persistence. It stimulated her in a new and unknown way.

"Nothing. Just to look at you. You're . . . special."

"Last time it was beautiful."

"Special and beautiful."

She needed the beautiful, even though she had declined his offer to spend the rest of the evening with him.

Danny and his goddamned snake!

She heard Man-Kit chuckling, somewhere in the distance, as she entwined the sheets around her legs in bed that night. Her only consolation was that she knew he was doing the same thing in his bed in Hong Kong.

It was five in the morning. Rosemary had slept badly, waking up every hour, tossing and turning all night. She got out of bed and took a drink of water.

She wanted to call Man-Kit, but knew that he'd be out with Sonny this afternoon. Besides, the telephone bill had arrived today, and the first of their long distance calls had shown up, much to her horror. There was no Manky now to soothe over the expenses, to juggle their finances in his usual, expert way.

And then, there was something about Danny.

Admit it, she told herself, you're hornier than hell.

An angry flash overtook her as she thought of Manky missing her, but not craving her the way she did him. Sex was a funny thing with him — it seemed he could take it or leave it.

She finished her glass of water and went to the bathroom to get another. The air was stiflingly humid; her sinuses reacted to the oppressive climate, clogging her nasal passages to an unbearable level. For the last three hours, she had fought a mounting desire to take a Sudafed. She gave in at last, and waited for the relief to set in as she sat up in bed.

The phone rang.

She grabbed it eagerly. "Manky?"

An unfamiliar woman's voice spoke, *"Hui siu je?"*

Hearing herself addressed by her family name, in Cantonese, took her aback. "Who's calling?" she replied in the same language.

"I'm your father's fiancée, *siu sing Chan,* humbly surnamed Chan."

Rosemary felt the tension mount in her. She loathed what she considered pretentious Cantonese humility, even as she recognized this woman's words as simply the polite language of Hong Kong.

"Do you have any idea what time it is here?"

There was a short pause, and then she heard an exclamation, "Oh, I'm sorry, I miscalculated the time."

It figured, she thought, that her father would pick some bird-brain to ease his post-midlife crisis. Her mother, an energetic, intelligent and educated woman, emerged in her memory. What an insult. She would be absolutely rude to this woman, Hong Kong rude.

"Please forgive me," she continued. "Maybe I should call back."

"Well, you've woken me now. What can I do for you?"

"I wanted to introduce myself. Your husband said he told you about me, and that makes me think you can't be too happy."

Despite herself, Rosemary began to soften a little. But she couldn't let her guard down that easily.

"Well, you're right. I'm not happy."

"Please understand, it's not money I'm after. Your father said you will get a green card soon, and that you could get him one too. He said that if I married him, I could get one and that way I could also help my family leave Hong Kong."

So that was it. She listened on, unwilling to bestow an easy sympathy.

"You won't believe me now, I know. Your father doesn't know I'm calling you. He would probably be angry if he knew. But you must understand that I sincerely respect your father. He's a good man, very kind but so lonely. He likes me and just wants a little happiness for his old age. That's not so bad, is it? A man likes to feel young by having a young woman. I'm not very clever or wealthy, but I'm young and quite pretty."

The woman had spoken hurriedly. Rosemary heard the fear and apprehension in her voice. It was a strange desperation, something she had seen in some of her ESL foreign students here in the States.

Taking advantage of the silence, the woman continued. "Your father tells me you haven't been back to Hong Kong in six years. Things are very different now. You wouldn't recognize half the buildings along the waterfront on both sides of the harbor."

"Miss Chan, are you and my father formally engaged?"

"We have an understanding."

Rosemary sighed. Things seemed so ridiculously out of control, so far away from anything she knew.

"I believe your father needs me."

"You've made him need you."

"Please, you're angry. I apologize. I woke you up. You can't be expected to know how things are here. In the last week, especially, since Tiananmen.

"My mother left China almost forty years ago. Her family were landowners. You know what that meant in China. My mother is seventy, but she still hasn't forgotten what it was like then. My father died in China; he couldn't get out."

Rosemary's head began to spin. Her sinuses had cleared, but this woman's words nagged at her, forcing her into an uneasy acceptance of her plight. It wasn't that she had anything to fear, but she did have a duty to her mother. Rosemary forced herself to speak politely.

"Miss Chan, my father is free to do as he pleases. Of course, if he wishes to marry you, I will give you the proper respect. And if my father wants me to get him a green card when I have mine, I will do so. You understand, of course, that my father has to ask me."

"Then, Miss Hui, although I should really call you Mrs. Ho, we understand each other. I'm sorry to disturb you. I will not bother you again. Thank you."

She hung up.

The entire exchange, carried on in Cantonese, had an efficacy that collapsed time. Six years was a long time to be away from home, to adapt to and adopt the milieu of the university and surrounding New England towns. She found herself picturing this Chan woman — an artificial Hong Kong beauty with too much makeup. But at least she had acknowledged Man-Kit's place in the family, and called her Mrs. Ho. Rosemary knew it had to be her father who had somehow conveyed that acceptance to Miss Chan.

A glimmer of light peeped through her bedroom window. She would be exhausted in class this morning.

V

Rosemary barely made it through class. Then, her best writing student from Cape Verde failed to turn in his assignment on time, and the only excuse she could get out of him was that he hadn't finished his research. He was writing about a national hero in his country, and could not let go of his draft until it was perfect because, he said, too few people knew about his hero. She gave him an extension.

Around noon, Celia, who shared her office, said, "Rough morning?"

Celia Wong was an ethnic Chinese ESL Education grad student from Jamaica. She and Rosemary had commiserated over many a coffee break.

"I'm too soft on these kids," Rosemary moaned.

"So why don't you be the mean teacher who accepts no excuses?"

"You mean, force Chinese discipline on them."

"Discipline isn't just a Chinese trait."

Celia, she knew, made the kids toe the line much more than she did. Their other office mate, an Irish-American woman who had grown up in Japan, was even stricter than either she or Celia. Rosemary decided she was simply not cut out for teaching. Her students' personal miseries had a habit of emerging during conferences, sometimes to the detriment of their lessons.

ESL simply did not strike her as a sufficiently serious subject to discuss compared to the problems of adjustment that plagued her students!

"Come on," Celia chided, "what's really bothering you, darling, or are you just missing Manky?"

Celia always called him Manky, never Man-Kit, and there was almost always sympathy in Celia's voice, colored by her musical Jamaican accent that Rosemary had come to like.

"I guess that's part of it."

Celia gathered up her books and papers into a tote bag imprinted with the logo of the local public radio station. "Well, whenever you want to talk, you know where to find Auntie Celia, if she doesn't find you first." She gave Rosemary a hug. "Got to go. Jamie'll be wanting his lunch," she said, referring to her four-year-old son.

Rosemary smiled at her. "Thanks."

It was late afternoon. Rosemary uncorked the bottle of wine and poured herself a glass. She undressed.

Manky, slender and sinewy, remarkably strong despite his slight frame, had been so extremely attractive to Hong Kong girls. She remembered the jealous stares of other women he knew when they had first started dating. And how she had reveled in that! Yet the only reason she had won him at all was that she was the first Hong Kong girl he had ever met who understood jazz. And, she knew, she was the only Hong Kong girl he had ever met who would accept the independent, solitary life he demanded then, putting up with the temperament and moods he hid behind the mask of his friendly, flirtatious, social demeanor.

What was Manky doing this very moment, Rosemary wondered. He might be cruising the clubs, looking up old friends, and maybe, she considered jealously, even old girlfriends. Despite the reason for his trip home, she knew he was more than likely enjoying the reprieve from America, and her. She sank her body into the warm bubbles in the bathtub, feeling slightly giddy from the wine she had been drinking, feeling Manky's invisible fingers caress the loneliness out of her soul.

"What a most extraordinary thing!" Celia flung her papers and books on the desk as she entered the office. Her scarlet blouse, with a large, multi-colored macaw on the back, screamed out in contrast to her pale jeans. "Really most extraordinary," she repeated.

"What is?" Rosemary watched Celia's entrance, amused, relishing as she always did the music of her accent and her customary flamboyance.

"Well this woman. In my class. She's from China and is giving Mandarin lessons to some young American kid half her age. He's asked her to marry him! And here's the best part — she's seriously considering it."

Rosemary felt a sudden stab. Surely it couldn't be . . . but, she reminded herself, there were many Mandarin tutors and students at UMASS. "Do you know him?" she asked as casually as she could.

"No, never met him. An-Mei's beautiful though — that's the woman in my class — so it wouldn't surprise me if some guy did fall in love with her. You know the kind I mean? The ones on some intent Tibetan quest who keep asking if their Mandarin pronunciation is correct?" Celia laughed, and her voice filled the room.

Rosemary couldn't help smiling. At any other time she'd have laughed along with Celia, who always made scathingly amusing comments about what she called "those other China watchers". Celia claimed to know only a "smidgin of pidgin Chinese", was more Jamaican than anything else, and loved to startle Americans out of their assumptions when they met her by answering their polite "about Chinese people" queries with "but darlings, why ask me? I'm Black."

"What's the matter Rosa-M? You're going all quiet on me."

It was difficult to hide anything from Celia. With her, everything was out front, no holds barred.

Celia shook her head. "Oh boy. I think it's coffee time."

Embarrassed, she half managed to tell Celia, as she knew she would, about Danny, of his unnerving presence and her physical attraction to him, especially in Man-Kit's absence. But she left out the part about how he pulled at something inside her, the jealousy she was feeling of An-Mei. That she couldn't explain to anyone, not even Manky.

"So you're wanting some," Celia said. "That's no crime. Hard man's good to find, you know."

"Oh Celia," Rosemary began to laugh.

"That's my girl, Rosa-M. You're taking all this way too seriously."

"But who wants to marry whom?"

"Who gives a shit? You know how these entanglements get confused, especially when you're dealing with a mainland Chinese! The point is, what are you going to do about it?"

"About what?"

"About . . . your 'problem'?"

"Oh that." Rosemary blushed.

"Cold showers," they said together.

Rosemary knew that Celia was, despite her stoic manner, someone with great empathy for the plight of others. Celia's had come to UMASS as a graduate student where she met and married a Black Jamaican poet. When she was pregnant, he had an affair with the wife of an English professor, a Swift scholar, a "classic case of misogyny derailed and Oreo cookie fantasy fulfilled, in one fell swoop — swift, eh?" In short, they eloped to Boston University where he got himself a poet-in-residency, and Celia was left to raise Jaimie on her own. No alimony. "Darling, a poet's money is like his sperm, ejected into the first available sewer."

Now, she worked as a teaching assistant and part-time department administrator while finishing up her PhD. Celia did not waste unnecessary sympathy on herself.

Driving home, Rosemary reflected on everything Celia said. Her real "problem" was that she felt silly, because she had gotten caught up in Danny's little head game for lack of anything better to do.

But what had surprised her was Celia's reaction to the whole "marriage" thing between Danny and An-Mei.

"Do you know how many of my female students ask me about gay and straight men who have offered to marry them, some for a fee, some out of the goodness of their hearts? Or how many of my male students ask me if I think it's okay if some American girl who has fallen in love with them wants to marry them?"

Rosemary knew that none of her students had ever come to her about such things. Her students came crying about emotional longings, deep-seated sadness, depressions brought on by the vagaries of fate, bitter sweet sorrows of homesickness. And she would let them cry, sure that the outburst of complaints was a sort of catharsis.

Celia's students, it seemed, came with solutions.

"But what do you say to them?" Rosemary had asked.

"The same thing. Don't ask the question unless you actually want to deal with the answer. Why ask? Immigration hasn't."

"And what do your students reply?"

"Oh, some go on about family honor, guys usually. Others waffle on about being caught. Some just want to know how to raise the money. And you know something else, not a single one of these foreign nationals, in my four years around this ESL program, has ever demonstrated a sign of suffering from some personal, ethical dilemma the way your friend seems to be suffering. You know what I've decided, Rosa-M? It's just simply not a question of ethics when the green card is the issue."

Did ethics, like people, adapt to a foreign culture, Rosemary wondered, as she pulled into her driveway.

At home, she put aside her dissertation and whirled into a frenzy of housecleaning. She plunged into every mundane chore she could find, any work that was Zen enough to free her from the confusion of thoughts and feelings.

It was two-and-a-half weeks since Man-Kit had left.

Any day now, she thought, as she dusted the baseboards, he would call and say that his father had died and that he would be home in a matter of days. And then when her Manky was back, everything would be right again.

They could even try to have the child they talked so much about.

She began to sweat. How good it felt to be able to sweat in cold New England. Manky was always incredulous that she never seemed to sweat, even in summer. To her, summers here were like winters compared to tropical Penang.

The phone rang. It was Man-Kit.

"Isn't it three in the morning?" she exclaimed.

"I know, couldn't sleep. Too damned humid and sticky."

He would not use air-conditioning. The perpetual air-conditioned indoor climate was something he detested about summers in Hong Kong.

"I'm listening to the one jazz program," he continued.

Any minute now, she thought, he would begin extemporizing, improvising. He had woken her often enough at three in the morning after a gig. Just to talk. He never expected her to respond.

"Surprising thing," he said, "I've realized how much I miss home. Hong Kong, I mean. Remember that house Ricky and Anna lived in, hidden by trees, right along the railroad track in Shatin?"

They were friends of Man-Kit, a Portuguese couple. Ricky had been a rock disk jockey on Radio Hong Kong's English language station. Anna was the personal secretary to some bigwig at the Hongkong and Shanghai Bank.

"Anyway, that house didn't cost them much in rent, probably because it was so inconvenient to get to by public transport. And hell was it noisy! Remember those dinners during which the train would rumble past? Anna said she set her alarm by the train."

"We were always too stoned around them to notice," Rosemary reminded him.

"We could live in a house like that, you and I, Rosa-M. We could. We wouldn't have any trouble working in Hong Kong. It wouldn't be like in the States. The hell with 1997. We'll take our chances with our own kind."

He was silent for a moment. Rosemary could hear him brood, could hear his private voice warning him that it was too late to turn back. Games were necessary.

He started speaking again as suddenly as he had stopped.

"By the way, I ran into Anna. She's eight months pregnant, and looks absolutely wonderful. They still live in that house. She says hi.

"You know, I played with Sonny during one of his rehearsals. Felt good to pick up the sticks again, even if it was rock. I stopped into the Jazz Club last weekend. You'd like the place. Thought about sitting in, but I chickened out. Pretty bad huh? God, I played better than any of those clowns. Maybe I just need to haul out the drum set again. I mean, that's why I had to go to America in the first place. Too little jazz in Hong Kong.

"And you know what? Why wait any longer, about children, I mean. I'll get that job, and we'll both be able to work legally. So we go to NYU, where that professor would love to have you part-time, which is what you'd like, especially with a baby. Besides, if we had had a kid before, all our immigration problems could be solved because he or she would automatically be a citizen!"

Despite all the contradictions, all the dissonance of Man-Kit's solo, Rosemary felt the anxiety and tension that had plagued her melt away as she absorbed his words.

"Oh Manky, do you really think so?"

"Sure I do. We make life difficult for ourselves, don't we? Americans always talk about taking control of their lives. Well, that's what we need to do. Be Yankee."

Her exhilaration swelled as he continued to talk. It was this rapturous sensation, this overwhelming joy that made her feel Man-Kit owned her. Although the past year had been unusually difficult, their life together constantly swung in this pattern of highs and lows. Always, always, Man-Kit would break the tension that would build between the two extremes. He made her imagine all possibilities.

His drum set, each piece neatly locked away in its case in the hall closet, conjured itself up in her mind.

"And you know what else? The hell with this family of mine. If they can't see that there's no future in Hong Kong — I don't care if they're too scared to admit it or what, I'm tired of always being ragged on as a pessimist — we do what we want. That's always pulled us through before."

She could imagine him, stretched out on his family's sofa with the phone to his ear, his forehead damp with perspiration. Round about now, he would take off his glasses, rub the lenses against his shorts, cursing out his myopic condition. If he were here, he'd comment on her twenty-twenty vision, either saying she was lucky to have been born in Malaysia instead of Hong Kong where everyone wore glasses, or simply placing his hand over her eyes and whispering, look, no fog.

"Of course it has," she assented. "It always has, ever since we rented that first, unbearably small room in that bitchy old woman's flat. Remember that?"

She heard him chuckle on the other end and wished she could see him, be with him, touch him. His shoulders were probably all tensed up, the way they always got when he was excited or under stress, and she wasn't there to massage them into relaxing.

"Hey Rosa-M, I don't really want to live in Hong Kong anymore. You know that was just talk, don't you? Everyone's scared here. Even Sonny admitted to me that he'd leave tomorrow if he could. Imagine! You know, Sonny doesn't have a passport, just a CI. He was born in China.

"These last days have been wild. Do you know, all kinds of people have marched and demonstrated for days over Tiananmen? Over a million, they said on TV, right here in Hong Kong. People stretched from Causeway Bay to Central."

Rosemary tried to picture the road by the harbor, with this long snake of people gliding along it. Hundreds, thousands of people. To her, it was almost unimaginable, unbelievable.

"You know who marched? Rick and Anna. They called and asked me to go. 'We may not be Chinese,' they said, 'but we're Hong Kong people and what China does is part of our future too.' And then, later, I found out my youngest sister marched. My sister! Miss Hong Kong society princess herself. Something happened here Rosa-M. Something you and I have never seen before.

"Then dad said something in private to me. There's talk, apparently, of Britain letting in a limited number of Hong Kong

British subjects, which means civil servants like dad might have a way out. But you'll never believe what he said — that the British wouldn't do shit for the Chinese.

"So he tells me that if something happens to him, I'm to get mom and the girls out to America, since he's convinced that neither of my sisters will ever meet a man good enough for them to marry and maybe they'll meet someone 'over there', as he puts it. He doesn't want them to go to Britain if we can help it, because, he claims, they'll be treated as badly as the Indians and Pakistanis. He made me promise. I did. Didn't know what else to say. I couldn't tell him what a long way off we still were from securing our own position."

Before he hung up, he added that his father's condition was worse, and that he loved her very much.

For the rest of the afternoon and into the early evening, she worked quite happily on her dissertation and forgot the housework. She did not think about Miss Chan and her father, or even about Danny. She did not eat dinner till almost ten o'clock. By the time she went to bed, she experienced a voluptuous sense of fatigue that she had not felt in a long time.

That night, she felt Danny's snake slithering up her leg, and awoke suddenly, startled by the urgency of the dream.

VI

But Danny did not go away. On Sunday, she went to the Midnite Lite with Celia.

Celia had not wanted to go at first, saying she had too much work to do, and that it would be difficult finding a sitter. But she had given in to Rosemary's cajoling. Rosemary wondered why she had been so insistent on doing this, why she needed Celia to anchor her.

As she drove to meet Celia at the club, Rosemary strained to see through the light drizzle of rain that blurred her windscreen. The hazy headlight glare captured the alternating darkness and light of oncoming traffic.

The club was quiet. Summer kept the audience away. Rosemary bought herself and Celia beers and sat down at a table. Joel came over.

"I don't see you for over a year, and bang, you're here twice in a month."

She smiled. "It's like that. Improvising, I mean."

"Who's your friend?"

Celia extended her hand. "Celia Wong. I hope you guys are good. Rosa-M drags me down here when I should be home working."

Joel laughed. "We're slippery as a snake." He glanced slyly at Rosemary as he spoke.

He was not going to let her forget this, for all his own reasons. "Hey, Manky sends his love."

"Tell him to come home quick. You look lost without him." Joel stood up. "See you ladies later."

Rosemary began to feel hungry. It was a good sign, because it meant she had also begun to relax. She thought about French fries and onion rings. The band started their first set.

"How did you come to like jazz?" Celia continued. "I would hardly have thought of it as a Hong Kong thing."

"Oh, I suppose because of insomnia. This DJ, Tony da Costa, would come on at eleven or midnight and play jazz on Saturday nights. I started listening to his program when I was fourteen and never stopped." She swallowed a mouthful of beer and added, "Besides, it was music to masturbate by."

Celia laughed. It was a deep belly laugh. Rosemary had never laughed like that in her life, but she could feel it resonate. Everything was going to be okay.

This was fun. This was like the old days when she hung out at jazz clubs with friends while Manky jammed. Back then, they never worried about regular meals or having to get up in the morning. They improvised. Life had an easy, natural flow. When Manky stopped playing, all that life ended, and, suddenly, they were almost as bad as their already professional friends back home who lived and breathed a clockwork regularity.

Celia nudged her out of her thoughts. "I think this is a friend of yours." Her head tilted towards a figure beside their table.

"Hello, Rosemary," said Danny. He had a beer in his hand.

She looked at him, and then at Celia. He was waiting to be asked to join them. When he was not, he pulled out a chair and sat down without being asked. Games.

"Hi, I'm Danny." He stuck out his hand to Celia, who shook it and introduced herself.

He turned to Rosemary. "So you girls out for a good time tonight?" It was a different pose. His voice was hard, edgy, aggressive. His face was unusually flushed. She thought perhaps he had drunk a lot.

"Where's your axe?" she asked.

"Didn't bring it. Nor the snake. Aren't you going to buy me a drink tonight, Rosemary?"

Rosemary disliked the agitation he created, but recognized the strong, if temporary, power this stranger exerted over her.

Celia sensed it too. She cleared her throat and said, "Anything going on here I ought to know about?"

"We're old friends, aren't we, Rosemary?"

Rosemary felt herself despairing. Why couldn't she think of something to say, something to ease the tension? She did that easily, automatically, with Manky, who owned her and had real power over her.

Her stomach muscles tightened. Suddenly, she wasn't hungry anymore. She looked at Celia, begging to be rescued.

"Aren't you An-Mei's friend?" Out of nowhere, it seemed, into the river of Joel's cool saxophone sound, Celia had dropped a stone.

"Why yes, how do you know her?" Danny's voice softened. Rosemary noticed he had smiled at the mention of An-Mei's name.

Celia continued. "She's in my class, and asked me to edit a translation for her. I remember seeing you with her when she came to pick up the piece."

"What was the translation?" Rosemary asked.

"The snake story." Danny and Celia chimed in together. They paused, and laughed as if sharing a private joke.

"Actually," Celia offered, "it was a dragon story, or rather a snake that became a dragon and created a gorge, called 'the gorge opened up by mistake'. It's an old Chinese tale."

"So tell. *Jin tian wan shang women dou shi zhong guo ren.* We're all Chinese enough here tonight." Rosemary knew Celia understood more Chinese than she let on. Under the table, Danny's knee brushed hers, stayed a moment, and moved away.

Celia complied. "It's the legend about the snake that became a dragon by drinking some magic waters. When he grew his scales and tail, he became very vain and wanted to head for the ocean where all dragons go. Every creature he met told him to go east along the river to the ocean, but he wouldn't listen because he thought the fish and tortoise who gave him advice too lowly for him. So he banged and crashed his way through the mountains, instead of following the river's path to the ocean. In this way, he opened up a gorge in the mountainside."

"What happens to him?" Rosemary asked.

Danny interjected. "The gods punish the dragon for the destruction he causes, and execute him."

"And the gorge?"

"It remains for eternity.

"Later," Celia added, "the people in the nearby mountain village called the execution point 'the subdued dragon pillar'."

Rosemary reflected a moment. "Typical," she remarked at last, "Chinese don't like individuality. I mean, after all, the dragon was just asserting a little of his own identity, wasn't he?"

The music swelled. "Maybe, maybe not. The net result is a gorge and a story," Celia said.

"Don't you like the dragon, Rosemary?"

Danny's words, uttered in a low, lazy drawl, made Rosemary shiver. She looked at him, and saw his sly smile of complicity, urging her to bend to him, or was it only her imagination, fueled by desire?

"She's not the dragon type," Celia interposed, "are you Rosa-M?"

Rosemary knocked back the rest of her drink, excused herself, went to the bar and bought another. Joel was still at it. His solo wrapped itself tightly around her; the sax head forced its stare deep into her, Manky's stare.

She heard Danny saying to Celia as she returned, "So what year were you born?" and Celia replying, "Dragon. A good, fertile year," and both of them laughing. Perhaps this was just good fun, something she wished she understood. Had her marriage to Manky really changed her to the point that she couldn't just have fun?

Celia stood up as Rosemary returned. Listen, I've enjoyed this but I've got to go. The baby-sitter will be getting impatient by now."

Rosemary almost rose too, but changed her mind when she saw Celia's face.

"Don't leave on account of me," Celia said. She leaned over and hugged Rosemary. "I didn't say when to take the cold shower," she whispered.

She watched, a little reluctantly, as Celia left, a grin in her wake.

"So," Danny leaned closer, "now that your friend has left us alone."

"But we're not." She edged away.

"What do you mean?" he demanded, staying his ground.

"There's An-Mei." As she said this, she suddenly understood the hold she had on him, which lessened his power over her.

He pulled back abruptly, his expression cautious. She knew he was trying to figure out how much she knew.

"What do you want to do, Danny?"

"Right now? Guess?"

She averted her eyes, embarrassed.

Manky's lips, on her ear, caressed her memory. Damn Danny and jazz and the beer she'd drunk! It wasn't fair. Life shouldn't insist on her making such choices.

Danny didn't move.

The music stopped. A feeble round of applause filled the club.

Joel walked towards her table.

"You weren't paying much attention to the music tonight," Joel challenged her, barely acknowledging Danny. "It's not like you Rosa-M."

"Blame it on the friends," she replied as lightheartedly as possible. But for just a moment, she heard Manky's voice, accusatory, from sometime in the past after one of his gigs, saying, "Why weren't you paying attention tonight?"

"Friends?" Joel glanced sideways at Danny and walked away.

"Come on," Danny took her hand as he stood up. "Let's get some fresh air."

They walked outside to the back of the club which faced onto a parking lot. The humid heat permeated her body. She and Manky had stood there often, smoking pot in between sets. Sometimes, she hadn't gone when Manky hung out with the other musicians, and remained inside the club.

Danny held onto her hand.

"Look," she began, pulling back, even though she wanted to follow him, wanted to yield.

"It's okay, Rosemary, don't say anything."

They stopped behind the club in the shadows, the glare of the street lamp missing them by inches. She was more than a little giddy now, the effects of the beer tingling urgently through her body. Danny's eyes laughed into hers, and his rich, resonant voice caressed her. Right now, this moment, she could take him anywhere, quite unafraid. It was a delicious sensation.

He gently positioned her against a wall, his long fingers on her waist. She felt his hands move slowly down the side of her body, sliding down her back. The thin jersey dress she wore crumpled easily to the sensation as his fingers pressed gently into her thighs. He leaned closer to her, his head bent forward. She felt his breath down the front of her dress.

She was inundated by his closeness, his delectably slow persistence. It was almost what she wanted. All she had to do was lean towards him and acquiesce to this tenacious desire that now threatened to overwhelm her. She parted her lips.

He suddenly pulled away from her, and stepped backwards into the spotlight of the street lamp, a pained look on his face.

Before he could say anything, she said, "Let's go back to my place."

Then, he stretched out his long arms, and took both her hands in his. He raised her hands in the air and kissed them lightly. "I'll go collect my stuff," he said.

Rosemary leaned against the cool, brick wall after he left. He could have had her right there, unresistant, against the building. A sudden flood of memories and voices assailed her — the encounters of the past fortnight with the still surreal Miss Chan, Danny and even Celia; the realization that her father was real, no matter how distant, as was her love and hatred for him; the persistence of her mother, so long buried from who she was and had become, evoked by Danny and his goddamned snake; Manky's absence, gnawing away at her, almost destroying her, despite the love that held them. She turned her face towards the wall and wept silently, unable to scream, unable to protest the horrible, empty feeling of abandonment that now engulfed her.

Her entire being was charged to a point she had never before felt with anyone except Manky. "Games," she murmured, to the summer's night air.

Speeding along the highway. Eighty miles an hour.

Rosemary had passed her apartment about an hour ago and was near Hartford. The cooler air earlier that night had degenerated into a stubborn, humid warmth.

Her body murmured an angry protest.

Damn Manky! Where was he?

She was coming up to an exit.

Get off, she thought.

She braked, too suddenly, and sent the car careening in an unmanageable swerve down the ramp. A chilling flash of isolation brought her to her senses, and she steadied the car at the bottom of the ramp, but not without hitting the stop sign at an intersection, jolting her forward against the wheel.

For a long five minutes, she sat in the stopped vehicle, unable and unwilling to move, shaking.

A spotlight startled her into calm.

The police officer aimed a flashlight into her face. Rosemary grimaced.

"You want to step out, Miss?"

She complied.

He trained the beam towards the stop sign. Rosemary saw that there was no visible trace of damage on the sign. She must have slowed down more than she realized, she thought, relieved that her natural coordination had taken over.

"Are you okay?"

She kept her eyes level with his chin. "Just a little scared."

"You must have come down that ramp pretty fast."

For a second, she felt the familiar anger rise within her as she heard Manky chiding her about her reckless speeding. But the feeling faded almost as rapidly as it emerged at the concerned tone in the officer's voice. She instantly felt immensely foolish and contrite.

He continued. "Have you been drinking?"

"Just a couple of beers."

He studied her face. Rosemary took a deep gulp of the damp air.

"I'm sober, honest," she insisted, her confidence returning.

He looked down at her wedding ring.

"What's the matter? Have a fight with your husband?"

"Yes, kind of."

He smiled. "Go on. Go home now. You don't want to be out here at this hour."

Rosemary slid gratefully back behind the wheel. She drove the speed limit the entire way home.

Danny was waiting at her doorstep.

"Are you okay? I've been here a couple of hours." The concern in his voice was sincere, kind. "When I came out of the club and you weren't there . . . oh, it doesn't matter anymore. Do you want me to go now?"

She touched his arm lightly. "No, come on in."

It was a little past five and the sky was starting to shed its blackness.

He followed her into the kitchen. She gave him a glass of water. Danny sat at the kitchen table. He said, abruptly, "You have the same last name as her. Well almost. You know, *gui xing Xu.*"

His Mandarin accent was quite good. Because of the slightly sheepish expression on his face, he looked even younger than before, no older than one of her freshmen students.

She sat down opposite him. "You mean your Mandarin tutor, don't you?"

He nodded. Looking away from her, he said "An-Mei's from Beijing. She's asked me to marry her." His eyes turned tentatively towards her. "We're not lovers or anything . . . though we could be if she'd let me," the last part rushed, as if an afterthought. And then, "You do look a little like her."

We all look alike, Rosemary almost said, but bit her tongue. She was using the phrase too much. She heard the boy speaking, vulnerable yet appealing. Annoyingly so, she realized, unable, even now, to stem the rising jealousy against this other object of his dreamy attention.

He continued speaking, seemingly unaware of the effect he had on her. "But she wants to stay here and I can help if I marry her. All the more reason now since June four. She's twice as old I am, and I very much want to help her. I don't know if I should do this or not."

He seemed in such a pained state. Rosemary believed him: it was An-Mei, not he, who instigated this idea of marriage. She felt an anger welling in her at the unfairness of what An-Mei was asking Danny, and also at the passion this woman seemed to inspire in him.

"In China, she was a student of Chinese literature. For a long time after she graduated from Beijing Normal, she worked on a commune in Northern China. She doesn't talk about those days much. Do you know what she's studying at UMASS now? Engineering. Can you believe that? She said it was the easiest way for her to get into the exchange program. But she loves literature and language. It's easy to see that.

"She has an illegitimate child, you know, a little boy. She left him behind with the father. Since they're not married, she could marry me and get away with it. Once she gets her green card, or better yet, her American citizenship, she can divorce me, go back to Beijing and marry him, and then she can bring her whole family here. She has it all worked out."

How much truth there was in An-Mei's story she didn't know, and didn't care to know. She regarded it with the same skepticism she had for Miss Chan's love for her father, yet felt a grudging empathy. Green card love was like that. Rosemary found herself wanting to take Danny in her arms, to comfort him, to love him passionately so that he could forget this pain, to forget this other Hui woman, this northern Chinese lover he so desired who was at least partially manipulating him for her own ends.

"Should I do it?" he asked, and his large eyes, liquid and beautiful, held her like a deer captured in a headlight, frozen for a moment before its frightened flight.

"How long have you known her?" she asked.

"Three months."

Rosemary did not immediately respond. Three months! But she had to be fair. He was young, and appealing to her for help. Her thoughts shifted momentarily to her own situation. She and Man-Kit had entered the country on student visas to study for their master's. He had since converted to a temporary H-1 work visa which he was hoping to use as a basis for his permanent residency, and she was still on F-1 student status as a doctoral candidate, although her time in the program was starting to run out. In fact, she sometimes believed that the only reason she was in a PhD program was to extend her visa in the easiest possible way, leaving the more complicated resolution of their long term status to Man-Kit. They had been too legal for Reagan's amnesty program, but not legal enough to become permanent residents. Man-Kit was still working out details with a potential employer in New York who had agreed to sponsor him. She knew that they were, in many ways, more fortunate than thousands of other legal and illegal immigrants in the country. And of course, they were from Hong Kong, not China, which made a world of difference.

But the uncertainty! She knew how awful it was, not knowing for sure whether or not a piece of paper would come through, a piece of paper that could change your whole life. And all the time, there were the stories of immigration raids in the middle of the night, nightmares of deportation, visions of having to leave and never being allowed to return.

She wanted to tell Danny, of course you must do this! You're empowered. You save her, so that one person, and maybe three persons in this case, could be freed of China's clutches.

But he was begging her judgment. She had to be fair, to him, and not to this unknown woman, this unknown "countrywoman".

"Three months is not a very long time," she said at last.

He stood up and began pacing her kitchen floor.

Why was he asking her? Because he did not reply, she asked, "Are you in love with her?"

He stopped pacing and stood very still in the middle of the kitchen. "Yes. No. Oh, who knows? Have I fallen in love? Is that what this is about? She cried, you know, after she told me about her lover and child, and I comforted her and put her to sleep. I'd never seen anyone cry like that. It was as if she were crying for herself and the whole universe. She frightened me. And yet the next morning, it's like we're strangers, like it never happened."

He sat down again, as if exhausted by his speech. Rosemary poured him more water. Life was moving too rapidly for her, at an almost manic pace.

She had seen some of her female students cry like that. She had listened to some of her male students pour out confessions of loneliness and need just like Danny. Her students came from all over the world to face the isolation of a less-than-fertile promised land. She knew why he was asking her judgment.

But Danny was smitten, or at least, vaguely in love with her too, the way he probably would be with any Chinese woman right now. It was the idea of a lover he wanted, one that would bring to life the jumbled learning in his head. Since he hardly knew the difference between China and Tibet, Rosemary suspected any Asian, not necessarily Chinese, woman would suffice. Manky's Vietnamese jazz singer flickered briefly across her mind.

He gulped his water. "Is this fair, Rosemary? Is this right? I've only ever wanted to do the right thing."

The right thing! How American. A luxury in a world where people measured their lives in terms of green cards, acquired by lies and deception, even marriage. Danny's handsome face was drawn and tired, though the pallor of his complexion now had a rosy tinge of excitement. His forehead was creased with a frown, setting his large, Caucasian eyes even deeper into his face. Against his dark brown, almost black hair, the green of his eyes was startling, even a little surreal.

He had been gazing distractedly around him. Now, he looked directly at her, and caught her gaze. He smiled. She looked away, embarrassed.

"How long has this been going on?" she asked.

He gulped more water. "A couple of weeks."

"I don't know you, Danny, " she replied, looking up at him. "I can't tell you what's right for you. It's a difficult thing she's asking of you, and an even more difficult thing you're asking of yourself."

His eyes lightened. There was a tenderness and openness about him she liked. It wasn't just pity or lust he elicited.

"Thanks," he said, calmer now. He reached across the table and touched her hand lightly. "I owe you."

The effect of his touch on her senses was powerful. She wanted to push his hand away, frightened by her desire for him. Yet all she would show him was a calm and composed face. "No you don't. That's what friends are for."

Danny stood up. He was remarkably lithe and tall, over six feet. The hairs on his legs and arms were a soft brown, not nearly as dark as the hair on his head, and they covered his skin like an airy layer of down. She could imagine his long arms encircling her entire body, and his legs between hers, the hairs caressing her skin. So different from Manky and his smooth, hairless skin.

"I've got to go," he said. "Goodnight, Rosemary. Thank you for not being too angry with me."

He left, a few minutes later, his glass almost empty.

Why, she wondered, was he so apologetic? It was almost six thirty. Time for Celia's cold shower, and then she would call Manky. And then perhaps she might be able to sleep.

She had wanted to call earlier that evening before going to the club, but didn't dare because it would be Sunday morning in Hong Kong when his family liked to sleep late. Manky wouldn't mind; he could be awakened from the deepest sleep and be alert in a matter of seconds. But her sisters-in-law, whose bedroom was closest to the living room phone, would assail her in their rapid Cantonese and ask if she were *chi sin,* crazy, to call so early. Since they each could no longer have their own bedroom with Man-Kit's return, they would be even less sympathetic to an early morning phone call for no apparent emergency.

How could they, single as they still were, understand the bond and necessary communication between husband and wife?

In Hong Kong, she could have lorded her married status over them. She would have given them *laisee* packets of lucky money at Chinese New Year, a gift given only by married persons and received only by single persons and children. And even her in-laws would have sided with her against their own daughters in any important family squabble. In Hong Kong, she would have been the adult as a married woman.

Here in the States, she felt more adult when she had been single, and more like a child as a married woman.

The sky was only just beginning to glow. Rosemary liked summer mornings. From the kitchen window, she could see across a field to the hills of the Pioneer Valley. Soon, it would be the season when all the trees ignited vales and hillsides with the fire of fall.

Autumn in New England was terribly soothing.

When she and Manky had first arrived at the University, they had lived in Amherst during their first two semesters. She had found that first fall semester a wonderfully calming time. Oh there had been the energy of new places, people, students, classes. But what she remembered most was the sense of freedom, of leaving behind the pervasive sense of restraint and disapproval that surrounded her affair with Man-Kit in Hong Kong. Neither his nor her family ever expressed anger, or ever were overtly rude to them. Yet she knew, as he did, that because they had been unmarried in Hong Kong, their families, and even some of their friends, would never fully accept their being together.

Even their marriage, celebrated with neither family nor friends present — they hadn't told either family about the wedding — had taken place because at the time, Manky had gambled on obtaining a J-1 visa from his H-1, which meant she could get a J-2 as his spouse, both of which would simplify their eventual applications for green cards.

Love, somehow, had nothing to do with anything.

The phone rang, insistent and loud.

"Rosa-M? I'm not waking you, am I?"

She almost cried in relief. Before she knew it, she was pouring out the whole, incomprehensible tale, about Danny, the Midnite

Lite, her drive to nowhere and most of all, the horrible feeling of abandonment at being alone and needing him so badly that her life was completely off center. As she spoke, she felt the customary surge of comfort brought about by Manky's soothing presence. Quiet now, he was saying, as the words tumbled out through her tears. It's okay.

I won't leave you again, she heard him say, and she calmed down, her emotions more firmly in check. As she dried her eyes with the back of her hand, she began to wonder why in fact he had called.

"Is your father . . . ?"

"He passed away this afternoon."

In that moment, she heard in his voice all the pain and bottled up sadness that demanded release. Yet there he was, calm, competent Manky, doing everything sensibly as always, comforting her instead, exhibiting no jealousy or anger, shouldering the responsibility of making their life continue.

The shock of reality calmed her like a spring rain, prodding her center into wakefulness, ensuring her survival.

"Oh Manky, I am sorry." She was more than sorry, feeling that she had let him down, that she had managed, as she often did, to grab center stage when what he was going through was so much more important. That her dependency and neediness hung heavily on him, preventing his necessary expression and release, until, too late, he would rage in anger at his inability to share his sorrow.

When he came home, she thought. Manky could explode when he came home. It was the only safe place for him too, she knew, picturing him calm, collected, while the rest of his family grieved.

"It's not your fault," he said. After a pause, he added, "I'm almost done with what I have to do Rosa-M. I'm coming home."

He told her he would take care of the funeral arrangements, and fly back to Massachusetts next Saturday.

VII

On Wednesday morning, Rosemary saw Danny again.

He was in the corridor of Bartlett Hall by the classroom where she taught. He was carrying his bari sax case, but no snake.

"I've decided about An-Mei," he said, as soon as he saw her.

The expectation in his voice! He was once again her student, begging her approval.

He didn't wait for her to ask. "I'm the dragon, aren't I? That's what she's been telling me all along. I have to sacrifice myself for her by taking the way I know is wrong."

How terribly idealistic he seemed. Yet his intensity persuaded her of the sincerity of his intentions. She wanted to ask him, and what about the music, or for that matter, the snake? Each of the faces he showed her seemed to disappear, as if her presence dissolved all these parts of him into nothingness.

Instead, she said, "Are you sure it's 'wrong'? Isn't the world full of dragons?"

They began walking towards her office.

"I'm selling my bari sax, by the way. To pay for my trip to China."

"When do you plan to go?"

"Soon. Once things are settled about An-Mei. I'm going to Beijing to tell him, the father of her child I mean."

"And your snake?"

"Oh that." He gestured vaguely. "I guess I'll figure something out before I leave."

She wanted to tell him that none of his "sacrifice" would be worth much if he didn't somehow come closer to the meaning of his existence. And that all the passion, all the desire, all the heroism of his shouldering this white man's burden would dissipate.

But he wasn't looking for advice.

He stopped short. "I've bungled everything, haven't I, with you I mean. That's typical though." He looked petulant and unhappy.

His voice had a virginal quality that made Rosemary instantly realize how ridiculously young he was. It had been up to her to seduce Danny if that had been what she really wanted. Of course he would bungle it; his intent had never been to seduce, merely to experiment with a feeling he liked but didn't understand. She remembered Manky, the night she had caught the Vietnamese girl kissing him at a party. How he had pushed the girl away as Rosemary came into sight, and run after her saying, "Please Rosa-M, it wasn't me." This wasn't the same. This had been her. She owed him.

She put her hand on his arm. No tingling, no sensation. "Danny Leyland," she said quietly. "You're going to be quite a dragon."

His smile was all she needed. "Will you remember me?"

"Someone once told me Rosemary means remembrance."

He walked her to her office door.

She touched his elbow. "Take care of yourself, Danny."

"I will," he said. Then, leaning forward, he kissed her cheek, and she whispered in his ear, *"Zai jian."*

Celia's infectiously warm grin greeted her. "Hey Rosa-M, what was that all about?"

"Oh, snakes and dragons, I guess," she replied, smiling a little dreamily. "Even dragons have to come down to earth in time. But we do say 'see you again', not 'goodbye', in Chinese."

Celia shook her head. "You're just too Chinese, darling," she said, a wry smile on her face.

Rosemary tried to stack her pile of papers on the desk. They slid into an untidy heap on the surface.

"You know," Celia observed after a short silence, "you're altogether too much in love with Manky."

"It helps me feel invulnerable."

"There's nothing wrong with being vulnerable."

Rosemary riffled through her papers. "Isn't there?" she demanded.

"But you're too hot blooded, Rosa-M."

"So is he."

"Then maybe you both just need to cool down, or something."

Rosemary grinned. "Come on, Celia. It's just summer."

On her way home that afternoon, she listened to the China news reports on her car radio. The fear had subsided, and a certain amount of resignation had set in. But, said the announcer, among the students, there still was hope. She did not switch off the radio. At least, she decided, the worst was probably over, although the tremors would prevail for a long time to come.

That evening, Man-Kit called. His father's funeral arrangements had all been made and would take place on Thursday. He would fly back on Friday instead.

That night she had a dream. She was sitting naked, except for an orchid between her legs, at the bar in the Midnite Lite. Man-Kit was jamming with Joel and the band. Danny was playing a solo, coaxing long, languid notes out of his bari sax, playing even better than he really did. Danny's snake, which was in its cage at her feet, slithered out and up along the barstool around her legs. It coiled around her waist, its head brushing the petals of the orchid. Its unblinking eyes held hers as it slid further up along her arm, and stopped at her left elbow.

And then, the snake glided off in a single, rapid motion, and writhed away across the floor towards the bandstand, towards its master.

Rosemary woke up. Her covers were in disarray. She got out of bed and stood naked by the window, sipping the glass of water she kept each night on her nightstand.

In two days, Manky would be home.

They would make love silently as they always did. And then, he would talk about his father. He would grieve at last, the way he hadn't been able to in Hong Kong, and cry like a child in her arms.

Then when the grief eventually passed, he would talk, with his usual impatience, about the rest of the trip and their life. He might complain about the company and the bureaucratic delay surrounding his visa. He might worry about his mother and sisters who, she knew, had no desire to move to America no matter what his father had said. He might say he wished they could take a vacation, and she might stifle her inclination to say not in the middle of the summer semester. He might tell her about all their old friends in Hong Kong, making her nostalgic, and say that he wished there were a realistic way for them to live there, at least for awhile.

They would even have a little fight, brought about by the tension of their time apart, after which they could make up and make love, perhaps without her diaphragm.

And Manky might actually take up his sticks again.

Hillsides and gorges opening up. Dragons in China.

It was starting to be light now.

The Pioneer Valley glimmered in the distance, green and lush. Rosemary pushed the window completely open. If only autumn would come. Autumn, with its crisp red falling leaves, meant a return to something sure and definite, something less shrill and edgy than the symphony of summer. Pieces fell into place during a New England autumn, as solid and firm as the pumpkins and gourds that crowded the vegetable stands along Route 9.

Even if nothing changed after Manky's return, the echoes of all that had happened would continue to resound for a long time. Now, the echoes of future feelings and words tumbled rapidly around her. Through this jumble, their joint destiny together slowly emerged before her as a winding river full of strange and yet undiscovered life forms. Shadows and sunlight zigzagged this way and that, obscuring the banks and waters, concealing the flow from her. Rosemary listened hard in the distance, trying to hear the murmuring message of the water, hearing only the sounds of a solo, long forgotten, a remembrance of an earlier jazz life. Merging sight and sound, she knew the meaning of harmony, the meaning of all those musical terms Manky had tried to teach her. Why he always insisted that music had to be experienced live, so that you could see, smell, taste and feel what you were hearing with all your senses. And then she saw it, the end of that river, glimpsed through a thin veil of uncertain mist which might, as long she kept her eyes trained on it, eventually lift and lead, one day, to the ocean.

Loving Graham

Why is Boston always so cold?

Sixty Minutes . . . oh, what the hell does *Sixty Minutes* know? They're saying it's almost the year of the ram in Hong Kong, a city on the verge of 1997 which is when China can reclaim sovereignty, and that people are now wary, mistrustful and running away. Take it from me — being Hong Kong Chinese was always about being wary, mistrustful and running away.

When will the heat in this apartment come on?

I'm tired. Alan can keep his house, his trust fund, his best friend and his ego. I don't care if he thinks that I seduced Norman or that I'm sick and amoral. You know, adultery with his "best" friend wasn't the worst thing I could have done. What did he expect? He was never around, and Norman was. I can't stomach any more of his New England moral and intellectual vigor. I miss Hong Kong. I want to go back.

Mother can cry her eyes out, but Alan will be there to commiserate, the way Philip was there to commiserate when he divorced me way back when marriage mattered even more in my life. My parents and my ex-husbands: the happier families.

Where is that divorce lawyer?

I just want something that feels a bit like love, if not marriage. Like loving Graham.

I met Graham Maitland in Hong Kong in the April of '79, exactly thirteen months after my divorce from Philip.

Alan and I were at a concert, Rachmaninoff, I think. Free tickets, of course, because the pianist was a rising young Vietnamese-Chinese star from Julliard, and the American embassy would want Alan Berman, one of the first American foreign correspondents in China, to be among the guests of honor.

I spent pre-curtain, intermission and post-curtain tagging along while Alan said hello to everyone.

Graham came along during intermission.

He was escorting an American client's wife, the client being in Tokyo that evening. She knew Alan and cornered him, and, after introductions — Alan's standard one for me being, by the way, she's Hui Man Ming's daughter — the two of them chattered away about the importance of Alan's upcoming assignment to Beijing, although I could see it wasn't his assignment she was really interested in.

Graham stared at me with his amazing gray eyes. I couldn't help staring back. He was tall — taller than Alan — and slender, almost thin, with wildly curly hair.

Long in Hong Kong what do you do? I asked.

Half a year merchant banking — and he named a small British firm which I knew.

I handed him my card in exchange for his.

He glanced at it and smiled — Chase Manhattan? Why?

Wharton, MBA — I told him, never taking my eyes off him.

How American of you.

Then I'll take it one step further. Let's do business, I said.

Yes, let's, Ms. Hui, he replied.

I was wearing a short, off-one-shoulder, crimson silk dress, and three-inch heels — the kind of outfit Alan complained was too showy. But I saw how he relished the jealous glances of other men when we appeared together in public. Philip was the same way. The slut factor.

Graham's eyes traveled all over me. Blatantly.

My body blushed.

And will you go to China with your friend? His eyes whispered the insinuation of his undertone.

You know I won't, I replied, and as soon as I said it he smiled in a way that told me he knew, saying, Then give me a call, sometime.

How could Alan have missed all that?

But then, Alan always missed things. Eight years of marriage and all his traipsing round the globe — surely he didn't think his catching me with Norman that once was the only time. I don't know what Norman told him. I tried with Alan, honestly I did. Once we moved to the States I stopped having affairs. Until Norman. What I don't understand is how I screwed up in almost exactly the same way twice. First Philip and his dear friend William, and now Alan and Norman. But best friends get reinstated with my husbands in a way that I can't.

Graham wouldn't have divorced me.

Where is that lawyer?

I might not have called Graham if Alan hadn't slighted him as a "pretty boy". Well, maybe that's not true. I probably was going to call Graham regardless. I still remember the sneer in Alan's voice, saying, poor Jane (or whatever the woman's name was), stuck with pretty boy when what she really needs is intelligent conversation.

How fortunate for her you were there then, I remarked, Yes it was, he replied in total earnestness, she really is an intelligent woman.

That did it.

Loving Graham

The day I called Graham, Alan was preparing for his fling with celibacy, which was what he called his pending assignment to Beijing. Alan was flurrying, which is his second favorite state, the first being flurrying in the midst of any major political crisis that would ensure a front page byline.

How marvelous that you did call, I'd been thinking of you, Graham said, Is your friend away?

I smiled into the phone and replied, Almost.

Although, he continued — and there was the slightest hesitation in his voice — I hear he's more than just a friend?

But that isn't what matters to you, is it? I replied.

I can't say why I knew, but clearly he knew I knew, because I heard that smile in his voice, the same callous, ice-cold smile I've seen on my face and heard in my voice whenever I'm about to do something that I'll apologize for, if I'm caught.

I think that was when I first had an inkling I could fall in love with Graham.

In fairness to Alan, Graham was something of a pretty boy. He could have been a fashion model, with his bedroom eyes and gigolo looks (I knew he had to be a good dancer, and he was). Even when he spoke seriously, he managed to sound frivolous.

Like about Anne, his ex-wife. An earl's daughter. Their marriage broke up when he was found dipping into clients' funds to expand his own portfolio. The real reason was that he had been sleeping with the wives of two of the partners at the London merchant banking firm where he worked. Which is how he ended up — in his words — banished to the colonies.

Graham told me this over wine and lunch the first time we met.

Mother was awfully upset, he said, a wry smile on his lips. She said she was glad Father wasn't alive to see it, since he adored Anne.

Everyone adored Anne, didn't they? I asked and then I saw that smile, and the pretty boy face vanished.

Maybe I'm wrong, since Graham was so long ago, but I think we fell in love with each other at our first meal. I remembered I giggled first, and then Graham chortled and finally broke into laughter. And then he said, your turn, and I told him about Philip Shen and the adultery with William Cheung but the public excuse was my announcing at a joint family function that I did not plan to have children, which I later followed up by sterilizing myself.

Well, I don't like loose ends, and I knew I'd make a lousy mother — I said — and I was fed up of mucking with birth control. Of course, neither his family nor mine saw things my way, and Philip is a family man.

Graham dipped his finger in the wine, anointed my lips and whispered — the silence of the damned.

Oh I know we were drunk and behaving shamefully. It was exhilarating. Somehow, in our silent pact, I knew he understood the really bad part of me, the part that could never love a Philip, or, as I know now, an Alan.

We were at that French place at the top of the Mandarin Hotel, the one where the menus don't even list prices, and I knew without being told that Graham was writing the whole thing off on his company's expenses, as he would all those expensive meals to follow, although he personally paid for the trip we took together to Bali. It was so refreshingly different from Alan, who was a tightwad, just like my father.

After all, I'm the kind of woman husbands love to be ashamed of.

Funny thing, my knowing this now. Must be age. I was twenty-five, and Graham twenty-nine. Alan knew he was wiser at thirty-three. Back then, I think I had an idea, but didn't know for certain.

Loving Graham

I remember the day Alan fell in love with me. We had just had sex on a Sunday afternoon when nothing was happening in China, during one of his trips to Hong Kong. I had been dating him for about eight months. He had met my parents who adored him, because he considered my dad famous, spoke Chinese fluently, had done Chinese literature and studies at Harvard and pretended that he and I were not engaging in premarital sex. The first time I stayed at his parents' house in New England, we slept in separate bedrooms.

Anyway, I was lying there thinking of Graham when Alan started tracing his fingers over my lips. Why do men always want to touch my mouth?

You have a sensuous mouth, he said. The first time I saw it, I knew it could, well, you know. And then, he told me he thought he could spend his life with me.

My first husband Philip was a lot less subtle — he was a press relations officer for the Trade Development Council. You'd make a great prostitute, he told me on our wedding night. And he meant that, sincerely, as a compliment.

The slut factor. That's what both my husbands wanted in marriage. They looked the other way when it suited them as long as I was discreet and they got what they wanted in bed. And I knew how to give them what they wanted. It was the same deal their so-called best buddies, and all those others in between, expected from me, as long as the boundaries of marriage remained. It's as old as the Great Wall: keeping civilization in check and the barbarians at bay. I guess I understand.

Why the hell doesn't the heat come on properly in this apartment?

Loving Graham is the one sane thing I've done in all my thirty-six years. He was the only man who pulled me up for air.

Graham and I didn't have sex more than three times in our eighteen-month love affair. And I think we did only because. . . .

Round about our fourth date — although being with Graham wasn't really like dating except in a teenage sort of way — he finally popped the question.

So why Alan?

My parents adore him. Dad especially.

Your father's a pretty famous intellectual, isn't he?

He was in China, once. He's something of an expert on modern Chinese literature before the Cultural Revolution. But you know how fame is — only as good as those who acknowledge it.

And your mother?

I let her down once with Philip. She's still not over it, especially the way it ended. I've told her Alan doesn't want children. But all she says is I didn't have to cut off my womanhood, and that I'm unnatural, and she didn't raise me to be a bad woman, and what kind of mother would people think she was? Besides, Alan's American.

Is America where your parents want to go?

Yes. That's why they sent me to the US to study.

They loathe the British, don't they?

No. They're pragmatic. Big pictures matter to them when it's expedient to do so.

And they left China . . . ?

With difficulty and hardship, of course. My mother and I came to Hong Kong first, and Dad did time being "reformed". He made a big sacrifice to ensure my liberty.

So what about Philip? Isn't he a British lackey?

He's Chinese. Racism isn't an exclusively Western thing. Besides, I've known him since I was twelve, and he did at least do graduate work in the US.

What about you?

What about me?

Poor baby, he said, and anointed my lips with wine again, only this time, he wasn't laughing at all.

Graham understood. His father, a consummate Royalist, had ensured his eldest son's Harrow-Cambridge career, ending in marriage to an earl's daughter. He showed me a picture of Anne once. She looked like Princess Di with longer hair.

My mother would give you tea, he said, a little wistfully.

But only as a passing visitor, right?

She means well, he replied.

They always do.

There's never been anyone like Graham in my life before him or since.

I'm not trying to blame my parents, honestly I'm not. They're good people, decent people, full of ordinary human fears. They just wanted the best life for their only child, and themselves. It's being my father's daughter that's difficult. Hui Man Ming didn't think much of statistics, finance and my MBA, which weren't "genuine intellectual pursuits". I'd be a better person to him if I were a poet and a scholar. But then, I wouldn't be in the position to take care of him and mother in case I didn't marry, and I am only a girl. My parents wanted a son, but Dad dried up after me.

I have looked after them though — I've always given them forty percent of my more than adequate salary as long as I've been working. Filial piety. Very Chinese, which is what my parents, and even I will always be, despite our Western-style lives. Alan understood.

Graham simply wouldn't have cut it in the parental scheme of things.

He said I had a great body and great legs which should be flaunted, at least on weekends. I'm tall for a Hong Kong Chinese woman, almost five foot seven, and I'm all legs. I would wear skin-tight mini dresses with nothing underneath and do the round of parties with him. And he'd wear an off white suit with a turquoise or orange silk shirt that practically glowed in the dark. On Graham's boat parties, I'd wait till everyone was drunk enough and lead the women in taking off bikini tops. People talked. I told Alan that people liked to talk and that Graham and I had a business relationship. Alan believed me, because he wanted to, because he wouldn't be caught dead with Graham's crowd anyway, because I said the right things to the right people about him, because I was a convenient fuck when he got time off from China. As long as I was there when he wanted me. And I was there, at Graham's expense, which was a big mistake.

The bottom line is that I really wasn't having an affair with Graham.

I was just in love with him.

It's crazy, I know, but Graham and I didn't care about the hallowed sex act. We just liked to tease. We'd drive out to the villages in the New Territories or to the beaches on the south side of the island at two in the morning, and feel each other up in the back seat of his Prelude. And he thought nothing of running his hand under my blouse or up my skirt in any semi private corner at a party. Once, at a dinner, he kept his hand up my thigh all during dessert. The very proper gentleman on the other side of me, who pretended not to see us, spent a rather long time in the bathroom afterwards.

Loving Graham is like plunging into the South China Sea at the height of the worst typhoon.

Alan was posted to Beijing for a year and a half. He came to Hong Kong every other month for a week, and wanted it badly when he arrived. He didn't want to get engaged while he was still in China, which was fine by me, although my mother found this distressing. I don't know why. She and my father were separated for seven years but remained true to each other, my mother never giving up hope and helping to engineer Dad's release. My father the victim of history, and my mother the worshiping wife. The perfect love. Alan was almost in tears when they told him their story.

My parents are a hard act to follow.

What Alan didn't know, or pretended not to know about were all the men I did sleep with behind his back. It was easy having affairs in Hong Kong, and I couldn't seem to help myself. After all, no one got hurt since no marriages broke up except mine, and that was only because . . . oh who knows why for sure? I guess Alan's right. I'm not cut out for marriage.

Graham helped matters. He and I procured for each other. I introduced him to a slender, almost anorexic English girl who waterskied beautifully and was married to the dullest Scottish auditor. Graham is as graceful on skis as he is on a dance floor.

Graham introduced me to his client, Jane's husband (I call her Jane because I never can remember her name). He met me in Tokyo during a conveniently arranged joint business trip. I felt a strange vindication screwing him while his wife's lust for Alan remained unfulfilled.

I liked procuring and enjoyed liaisons that required discretion. So did Graham. After all, that's more or less what we both did for a living. We introduced people, made money for people, found money for people — discreetly, without any fuss or bother, without asking difficult questions of morality — for a price.

But ultimately, I'll pay — or so Alan says — just like I'll pay for being promiscuous.

I don't deny I was promiscuous. Jane's husband wasn't the only one. Alan probably knew but pretended not to. Oh, Alan knew. The day he told my father he wanted to marry me, my father approved saying, good, maybe you can settle her down, and they both laughed knowingly, while my mother simply looked puzzled.

With Alan and Philip in Hong Kong, there didn't seem to be any other way to be. Life was one constant race, like the horses at Happy Valley racetrack, and my husbands had to win or place. I was the long shot. Then there were their confirmed bachelor "best friends," whom they asked to take care of me while they scurried through their frenzied, successful careers. Norman hung around me with hungry eyes in Alan's absence, having spent his life in Alan's shadow. And William? William said he and Philip went to their first prostitutes together, and that they shared all their women.

I wish that lawyer would get here with those divorce papers so that I can get this marriage over with.

I should switch *Sixty Minutes* off. Norman used to come over for dinner and watch *Sixty Minutes* with me when Alan was away, and what with the wine and the fact that I was bored and lonely and homesick for Hong Kong, Norman did the trick.

Sixty Minutes is such a joke. They go to Hong Kong once and do this great in-depth story on the psychology of the Hong Kong Chinese *vis à vis* the 1997 changeover. They should interview my father in California — he would love that. Oh yes, Alan did a great job stage managing their immigration. Pulled all the right strings at the consulate to speed things up, even got Dad a part-time position teaching Chinese at Berkeley — to make him feel important again. Philip, dear boy, is taking advantage of the Canadian government's immigration point system to qualify for his visa.

Hong Kong British though he is, he wouldn't be caught dead in Britain.

I think England would be rather nice.

I wish my father had sent me to Cambridge instead of Penn, although he'd sooner disown me than have done that. Besides, he had to pull strings through the US-China Cultural Exchange, where he worked as an assistant administrator, to get me scholarships for which I am grateful, since I otherwise couldn't have afforded college abroad.

I like tea. Boston's weather is no better than London's, which is where, I imagine Graham probably is now. Oh Alan tried. He made sure I'd settle right in here with a decent job at First Boston and all, but the only reason I came is because of him, because somehow, marriage was still important then even if monogamy was a bore, because at least my parents approved of me for a little while.

Now that things are clearly over between me and Alan, I should go back. Everyone's leaving, so there are plenty of jobs. I don't need to run away from Hong Kong. Communists, colonialists, capitalists — what's the difference? It's not the system that counts but surviving the system. The desperation *Sixty Minutes* keeps associating with Hong Kong people and our political future ... isn't desperation most of what life's all about?

But all this politics and sex stuff has nothing to do with anything. I've listened to endless debates and discussions by the likes of Alan and my father about politics. And I've endured as many of Alan's lectures about sex and morality as I can possibly stand. With Alan, it was always imperative to work towards mutual satisfaction during lovemaking. Once he got over the novelty of being married to a bad girl, he wanted sex to be some ultimate expression of love, and dragged me to three different sex therapists to sort out my "problem". I think that was when I began to come apart.

Boston has not been the liberating experience Alan assured me it would be. You see, Alan didn't accuse me of frigidity until we moved to Boston.

Graham knew from the start I was frigid, just like I knew he was impotent. He could only get excited enough to have sex after hours of foreplay, which made him a great one night stand with other men's wives. I hardly feel a thing during sex. Which was why he could turn me on with his teasing and games, while Philip and Alan and the slew of others couldn't do a thing with me. He didn't put much store in the sex act itself, just in all the trappings around it. It was the way I liked it, the way I truly experienced the physical pleasure that Alan couldn't coax out of me, despite all his forays into Freud, Jung and the *Kama Sutra*.

Besides, Graham wasn't impotent around me.

He told me Anne told all their friends that three doctors had said the reason she didn't get pregnant had nothing to do with her. He didn't blame her though, anymore than I blame Alan or Philip.

Alan wasn't completely deceived. He asked me once how I kept myself amused in his absence. I told him I had friends, but said I waited for him. He liked that. The funny thing was that Alan liked me to be independent, especially in having a lucrative job and knowing lots of people. But he was horribly jealous of Graham. I suppose he was right to be jealous. I could have left him for Graham.

But the fact is Alan preempted me. We almost didn't get married because of Graham. This was shortly before his stint in China ended in '81, after which he was going to be based in Hong Kong.

He said he had serious doubts about our future together because we were too different. He pointed to Graham as the prime example of that difference. I simply wasn't sufficiently serious which, he was quick to point out, he couldn't understand since my parents were the most cultured, intelligent and wonderful people he knew. Why I persisted in adolescent outrages with the likes of Graham was beyond him. It wasn't proper, especially in Hong Kong — couldn't I see that I was even beginning to suffer professionally? Graham was a poor business relationship to cultivate. Why couldn't I consort with the likes of Jane and her husband? As president of the Association of American University Women, Jane knew all the right people.

I chose not to point out Jane's husband's idea of consorting.

So, Alan concluded, it was best if we cooled off for awhile — of course we'd be free to see other people — and see how things worked out.

He told me this right after the evening I was late for a dinner with several of his important friends, Jane and husband included, because I'd been out that afternoon on another of Graham's boat parties.

I didn't stay with Alan that night.

Instead, I hailed a taxi and went straight to Graham's flat.

It's over, I told him.

He stared at me with his amazing gray eyes, almost, it seemed, in disbelief.

But your parents?

They don't know yet.

He smiled that smile and said, then let's go to Bali before they find out.

The first time Graham and I had sex was in Bali. It was like Eden there. The beaches stretch out along miles of blackish sand, and at sunset, the skies scream with scarlet fire. Graham found us these huts right on the beach, away from all the resort hotels. And then he bought us magic mushrooms, the natural LSD kind, and after a bowl of magic mushroom soup I was flying along the nudist beach where only the European tourists go.

Sex was an afterthought.

All through my psychedelic high, Graham laughed and called me his Alice, his pretty girl. It was a comforting feeling, being in Wonderland. We were naked on the beach, and all that sex stuff was as faraway and remote as the North Pole. I couldn't imagine doing anything like that with Alan or Philip. Alan meant being serious and sensual and real, all of which weighed on me like an albatross rotting in the sunshine.

I can't even remember whether or not I had an orgasm.

Coming back to Hong Kong was a downer. My mother cried for days, saying that I was ruining my life all over again and wasn't once with Philip enough? She said I was stupid and worthless despite all my advantages, advantages she never had, and how could I let a wonderful man like Alan go?

My father was stern and silent. He's a lot like Alan, stoic to a fault, with a strong sense of moral outrage when it suits him. It was his years of suffering in China as the uncompromising intellectual that did it, separated from my mother and me in Hong Kong, that he's held over my head all my life as if I were to blame. When he lashed out at me, it was about Graham. My father had heard, from Alan of course, about Graham's financial misstep that brought him to Hong Kong in the first place.

I could tell they would not be open to the idea of meeting Graham.

Graham was wonderful to me during the aftermath of my break up with Alan. He spent all his free time with me. I remember he bought me a deep green silk dress with a low back. It cheered me up marvelously when I tried it on at his flat. Alan didn't believe in indulging my wardrobe. Graham also sent me a dozen orchids every week for three months. I know it was silly and extravagant and frivolous. But he made me feel good for who I was, not for who I was supposed to be in my career track MBA position, or as the socially responsible future wife of Alan Berman, or as the daughter of Hui Man Ming.

Those were the happiest months of my life.

Why did marrying Alan matter so much to me?

You need him, don't you? Graham said.

To immigrate you mean? My father could set it up if he tried.

But he wants you to do it, doesn't he?

I could try through my job.

You and how many others? Besides, you need him for more than that, don't you?

We were sitting on his roof in our swimsuits eating raw, sliced tomatoes. He was right of course, the way he always was. I couldn't really arrange anything through my job. I didn't have the wherewithal. I've always gotten by because I cater to just enough of the right people, not because I have any strength of character and certainly not because I have the courage of any convictions, the way Alan or my father have. Besides, I knew, although my parents didn't, that I was beginning to slide off track professionally. I could probably coast for a long time, especially if I continued to cater to my base of clients, the ones who needed a veneer of respectability to shelter the profits of their questionable activities. The bank didn't care, as long as their end was legal. I couldn't take my job seriously, investing all that money for people who had too much of it to begin with. What did it really matter if the market was going up, down or collapsing?

You're on the verge, Graham said.

I wish I weren't.

Graham was silent for a long time, over an hour. Finally — Make up with him.

But that means. . . .

He took both my hands in his and kissed them. Don't cry my love. We've had our honeymoon, he said.

We stared at each other for a long time, and his gray eyes were warmly liquid like the hot springs of Java. Just him and me, with me on the verge.

He finally made love to me at around five in the morning. He was gentle and considerate, almost as earnest as Alan. It was different with Graham, though. Better. I didn't have to work for his approval.

So I gave Graham up. It took more than half a year to bring Alan around. What I had to go through! He "reformed" my wardrobe — by this time, he called my clothes indecent, not just showy — and dragged me to every serious lecture and cultural event he could find. I had to promise not to see Graham anymore, a promise I broke only once. But Alan came round in the end because he couldn't stay away. The slut factor. Works every time.

Why did Graham let me go?

Graham was eons ago. He married the waterskier who left the Scottish auditor. His marriage didn't last either; his fault, naturally. He got caught with a client's wife while staying at the man's home in Singapore. The story flew to Hong Kong's financial community since the man was well known, and his wife liked to kiss and tell. Alan delighted in telling me all about it. This was about two years ago. I don't know what happened to him after that.

What's so damned important about marriage? About family? They haven't anything to do with love.

If that attorney doesn't get here soon, or the heat come on properly, I'm going straight to Logan International and getting on board the next flight to Hong Kong.

The last time I saw Graham, it was purely by chance. We were at the Equatorial Hotel in Kuala Lumpur on business. It was shortly before I was to move to Boston.

I've missed you, he said.

Me too.

Will you like Boston?

I doubt it, I replied.

It's awfully far away, from everything you're used to, I mean.

I'll have to be good then, won't I?

Will you be good for long?

I don't know. How about you?

I doubt I'll have the courage, he said.

Alan has tons of courage. He won a Pulitzer for his outspoken reports on the conditions in China. These days, he's interviewing my parents and all their friends who left China and Hong Kong and are safe in America. The ones who now want to "speak out". He'll probably be acclaimed, at least by the American press, for reporting the outrage that the British government is perpetrating on Hong Kong as 1997 approaches. My parents are proud of him and ashamed of me. I've apologized to no avail.

The last night I spent with Graham, he said, Let's go for a swim, Ms. Hui.

It was around four in the morning. We had hours ago called our spouses to say we were turning in early. We had also finished two bottles of wine over the sexiest dinner I'd had in a long time.

The air was about eighty-five degrees, and the water in the pool wasn't a whole lot cooler. I stripped and dove in. Graham followed. And there under the water, minutes before the security guards scurried out with their flashlights, Graham entered me and made me burst with the pleasure that Alan could never make me feel.

So maybe I don't know about marriage and never will. Alan said so. But he also said I couldn't love, because I was shallow and amoral and didn't have the courage or selflessness to know what truly matters in life.

He's wrong, you know. At least about the love part.

The Stone Window

I

The second week of his holiday in Greece, Ralph Carder saw her sketching at the port of Kea.

She looked curiously out of place: a young, Oriental woman — Japanese? mused Ralph — among the fishermen. Ralph noticed her early in the morning as he set off to explore the island. At noon, when he returned to the port, she was still there at the café, sketch pad and pencil in hand. He wondered whether she had sketched all morning.

In the evening, after a swim and shower, Ralph did not see her at the port. Sunset was resplendent. The division between sea and sand, so ordinary by day, was sharply delineated by the red glow. Ralph walked along the beach till nightfall. Kea *was* perfect, a haven compared to London, an island treasure to which he must return.

The next day, he saw her talking to an American couple at the taverna. As before, her long, black hair was tied tightly in a ponytail. He thought of joining them — they were among the few visitors who dribbled into the autumn off-season — but hesitated. He was not yet so bored as to need the company of Americans. Of course, the Oriental woman might not be American. He glanced at her again. No, not American. Her gestures, small and contained, were decidedly Oriental (perhaps Korean, he reconsidered). But he shied away, preferring his English reserve.

By evening, the solitude had become oppressive. Athens and Crete, where he had spent the previous week, were livelier. More — how he hated to admit it — touristy. It was all very well sniffing the freshly baked bread, exulting in the scenery, contemplating the silence. But it did get horribly dull. At dinner in the taverna, he struck up a conversation with the American couple.

The husband was an architect, as was Ralph. They were retired, unpretentious Midwesterners who had sailed in on their yacht.

"This is real near the mainland," explained the man. "Makes navigation easy."

Their yacht was quite luxurious. Ralph joined them on board for a brandy after dinner.

"There's Philomena," said the woman, peering towards the shore.

"Who?" asked Ralph.

"That artist from Hong Kong. You've seen her — the only Chinese around here. She's always got a sketch pad with her."

"Oh, yes," Ralph muttered, straining to see.

"Wonder what she sees in him," the wife said.

Her tone, acid and almost angry, struck Ralph. He saw the offending man: a middle-aged, white-haired, pot-bellied man. Philomena and he were with a group of men.

"Why do you think she's with him?" Ralph asked.

"She said she lived with a Greek man. Her — what was it she called him — her benefactor. I don't know what she meant."

"How odd," said Ralph.

The conversation shifted to another topic. Ralph had a vision of Philomena in an orgy with all those Greeks. Artists, he thought, they were like that. Later, back in his *pension,* he found it hard to sleep.

The American couple sailed out the next day, and he was again at loose ends. Perhaps Kea was a mistake. He had expected an idyllic spot, away from the usual crowds, where he might meet a different sort of traveler. But everyone, it seemed, sailed in on their private yachts, and stayed around the port. Only he ventured inland, testing his limited Greek, waiting for the ferry scheduled three days hence to take him back to Athens.

He had been walking uphill for almost an hour when he came across Philomena perched on a rock. She was wearing black shorts and a black cotton blouse, and looked young, perhaps in her early twenties.

"Hello," he said.

She glanced up, shielding her eyes, but did not respond. Suddenly, like a cat, she twisted her body and slid onto the ground. Her lean, brown legs stretched out under his gaze. He sat down next to her. "What are you sketching?"

She stared straight ahead and snapped her sketchbook shut. "Why do you want to know?"

Ralph felt the sting of her rebuff. I'd like to slap her across the mouth, he thought. The violence of his reaction startled him. He was normally a calm person. "I'm just being sociable."

"Is that what you call it?"

There was a slight British inflection in her accent. She didn't move, and did not look at him. Ralph found his gaze fixated on her bare legs. Her skin was smooth and completely unmarked. Even her feet, clad only in sandals, seemed delicate and untouched by the roughness of the landscape around her. Like a child's.

He decided to try a different tack. "You're an artist, aren't you?"

"Yes."

"Oils, watercolors, charcoal . . . ?"

"Oils."

"And has life been good here with the benefactor, Philomena?"

That got her attention. She looked directly at him instead of straight ahead. "You disapprove?"

"Should that matter?"

She jumped to her feet in a single, swift, easy movement. "No." She began to walk away.

"Then will you come out with me?" he called after her.

She gave him a quick backward glance, but continued walking. "Come to my studio," she said. "Your body's not ideal, but it will do for posing." And she disappeared down the hill and around a corner, out of his sight.

He felt rather silly over the whole experience. What had possessed him to call after her like that? That had been a waste of time. He stood up, and brushed off the seat of his pants.

In the evening, he walked along the beach and noticed the house for the first time. It stood atop a hill at the southern end of the beach, and had a stone window. He moved closer to make sure. It *was* a stone window. Odd, what good was a window one couldn't see from?

He remained at the foot of the hill, puzzled.

A shout startled him. The doors of the house flung open, and people streamed out onto the patio. It was then he noticed another odd thing. The entire house was made of stone, of large, roughly hewn blocks. It was the only one which did not have the smoothly whitewashed walls of all the other houses around it.

"Ralph! Come up here and join us," Philomena called from the patio. Next to her, leaning against the railing, was the fat Greek.

Her whole demeanor had changed. She was wearing a bright yellow dress, and her long hair was loose. She was smoking.

He went towards the house, wondering how she knew his name.

Philomena took him by the arm and kissed both his cheeks in greeting. She looked older. Ralph realized it was probably because of her makeup. She introduced him to the fat Greek, whose name day party it was. Ralph quickly found himself surrounded by laughter, dancing, food, and *retsina*. It did not take him long to get drunk. A large woman in black danced up to him, tapped his cheek, and said "English!" to everyone's delight. He lost sight of Philomena for a couple of hours.

When next he saw her, it was in the room with the stone window at the back of the house. He found it hard to keep his eyes off her thighs, which flashed at him through the slit in her skirt.

She said, "This is where I paint."

"But there's no light in here." His words, he realized, were slurred by *retsina*.

"There's a window."

"A stone window," he said, and suddenly thought, how ridiculous I sound. And all he could think of was *I have to hold her, I have to touch her. . . .*

They embraced, and the sensation of her bare arms against his was cold. Then they were back in the midst of the party, and she was dancing with her benefactor.

In the morning, he awoke alone on the patio. Someone had thrown a blanket over him. He was naked. His clothes were strewn on a chair beside him.

The benefactor was standing in the doorway of the house.

"Kali mara," he greeted.

Ralph sat up, head reeling, and mumbled a reply. The Greek laughed. He continued speaking, too rapidly for Ralph to understand. But Ralph caught "Philomena" and *"kala!"* and wondered whether his reference to beauty was for her, her painting, or both. As Ralph got dressed, the benefactor held up both hands towards him as if he were holding an invisible blossom. Ralph thought he said something that sounded like, "Philomena, *kalaki-moo."* Not till he returned to his pension did he realize that perhaps the man might have meant "Philomena, my little doll."

For the rest of his stay, he did not see Philomena alone again. The benefactor seemed to be around all the time. On the last morning, Ralph awoke with an erection, having dreamt he watched Philomena and the Greek fucking, while all the time the Greek laughed and laughed.

Two years later, when autumn had made London's weather tolerable, Ralph was struck by some paintings in a gallery window off Upper Grosvenor Square. A watercolor, in particular, stopped him long enough to go in. The background had to be Kea, nowhere else. But the foreground was a conglomerate of buildings and faces, buildings *with* faces, he realized, upon closer inspection. And the colors seemed limited to gray and scarlet, although he was sure some hint of green or blue washed the scene.

The proprietor approached him. "Would you care to look at that more closely, sir?"

"Yes, please. Who's the artist?"

"She's Chinese, and signs herself by her surname, Hui. A rather elusive middle-aged woman who lives in Greece. It's the only piece of hers we've got."

Ralph continued to study it. It was surprisingly compressed, and the faces were Chinese. Philomena had said oils. But this painting had to be hers. It had to be.

He bought it, because the price was reasonable, and because it was just the right size for an empty wall in his flat. There the painting hung, undisturbed, for several years.

II

Fall in Athens was infinitely better than fall in Boston, thought Hui Sai Yee, as she sipped a grainy Greek coffee on her first morning in Syntagma Square. It was early, before eight. The adjacent coffee shop had not yet opened for business. Or perhaps, she thought, it had closed for the season.

"Philomena? Philomena Hui?"

The voice, and the hovering figure, gave her a start. She thought at once of the saint, the virgin martyr. But then she recalled Philomela, the tongue-less nightingale, from her readings in mythology.

"From Hong Kong?" the man continued. "Don't you remember me?"

He was Greek, middle-aged, and pot-bellied. His face could have been handsome, but was badly scarred by pockmarks. It was a good pick up line, she mused, as he sat down, uninvited.

"I am Constantin," he declared.

"I am American," she replied, "from Boston. Philomena and I are not related."

He ordered two cups of coffee, all the while looking at her. She did not protest. It was amazing, she thought, how readily people sometimes made themselves at home around her. Her Grandma who raised her in America often complained that too little bothered her.

"You look just like her," he repeated. "The same long, black hair, and those sloped eyes. You are small too, like her."

She didn't say all we Chinese look alike, and resisted the temptation to say was that all Greeks did. When she didn't respond, he continued talking, quite unrestrainedly, as if he had known her for a long time.

In a minute, she decided, she would leave him to see the Acropolis. After all, she wasn't here to be picked up.

"What are you doing here?" Constantin asked.

It felt like an omen, at least Grandma would have described it as such, that a stranger could inject into his commonplace question the problem of her existence. A year ago, she would have replied quite casually, I'm a stringer for UPI. Yet here she was, thirty, living off savings, of no fixed abode or profession, by her own choice.

"I'm a writer," she replied. What the heck, she'd have to begin saying it sometime. Grandma's voice cackled in her memory: You want to write stories? I'll tell you about my life in China. Why go to Greece to write? What's in Greece?

Constantin's eyes lit up. "Very good, very good. Our country is good for writers. Listen, I'll buy you coffee, and tell you the story about Philomena, and then," he struck his hands together twice in a gesture of dismissal, "that's all. I don't ask for nothing."

His English was remarkably good. No harm in listening, she decided. The Acropolis was probably still closed. She was sure he was doing *camaki,* though with more imagination than most. But then, this was Syntagma. Adapting was part of her style.

"First, I must show you something." He pulled out his wallet, removed and unfolded a sheet of paper. It was a sketch of a house on a hill.

She glanced at the picture. "What about it?"

"Look at the window."

At first, it had looked like the side of an ordinary stone house with a window. But now, as she looked more carefully at it, she saw that the window pane was shaded to match the markings of the stones. The effect was disquieting.

"It looks," she said, "like a window made of stone."

"Exactly!" He folded up the sheet. "It took me a long time to realize what she meant when she said, 'Inside, I see light, but from the outside, it is dark.' Anyway, Philomena Hui is an artist from Hong Kong. And she lived in this house on one of the islands."

"How did you meet her?"

"Listen," he held up his finger dramatically, "do not interrupt me, and I'll tell you. She was a crazy, crazy woman. Like a little child. After she left the man who owned that house in the picture, she lived alone, on Hydra, I think. I told her she needed a man to look after her, and she got angry at me. Imagine! She got angry a lot."

She was about to ask him another question, but he signaled her to be silent.

"My wife divorced me seven years ago. Now, I am a gambler. Well, I am a souvenir shop owner, but I gamble away profits." He made a shrugging gesture with his hands. "For seven years now, I have been alone. It's a terrible thing for a man to be divorced in Greece with no wife to look after. But you wouldn't understand about these things. You are too young, like her. I would have stopped gambling for her."

As she listened to him, Sai Yee could hear Constantin saying to Philomena — you need me, you must need me, because I am a man. Was Philomena, if she ever existed, really crazy? She was dubious.

Constantin continued at full momentum. "Philomena came one day to my shop and bought some pottery. She wanted to send these to Hong Kong, to her parents, she said. From the beginning I told myself, 'Don't bother with this woman.' Something about her was not quite right; she behaved like a bad woman, even though she wasn't."

"What do you mean?"

"I saw her many times alone, in the Plaka and Syntagma. Everyone talked about her, everyone knew she was a bad woman. Only I knew she wasn't."

"But why do you say she was 'bad'?"

"You know, too many people talk talk talk about her. Said she went with many men. Said she was crazy. She stayed in a little hotel in the Plaka by herself."

Perhaps, she thought, she had made a mistake listening to him. He seemed a little crazy, and Philomena sounded too mysterious to be real. But this had to be some kind of love story, and it aroused her curiosity. "What happened between you?"

"I took her to a gambling house, but only because she insisted," he added quickly. "You understand, I'm a respectable man, even though I'm divorced and a gambler. I don't take ladies to bad places. You wouldn't go to one, would you?"

"I don't gamble."

"As I said, you wouldn't go to one."

What was it he objected to in this Philomena that made him say such curious things, she wondered. He obviously didn't seem to expect much response from her, as if her questions interrupted something that didn't warrant questioning.

He continued without pause. "And she gambled crazy. Put all her money in — they played blackjack there. Didn't even wait for me to introduce her, to explain that she was just a tourist who wanted to see the place. She spoke Greek too, which I didn't expect, and won plenty. Then she stopped, just when I would have continued playing. I asked her later why she stopped, and she said, 'I have a fixed amount in mind that I can win or lose. I am not interested in gains or losses, just in maintaining a balance. It is important for my *wa.*'"

The way he said it sounded more like *"hwa"* and she wondered if he were saying the Chinese word meaning harmony or peace.

"Philomena stayed in Athens for a couple of weeks. I offered her my home, tried to make friends with her. But she was unfriendly. Only one time, we went to dinner together, and then she insisted on paying. Here is the strangest part: she paid for the meal with a gold American Express card."

He waited, clearly expecting a reaction.

Perhaps he was mad, she thought. "Many people have credit cards."

"But Philomena was from Hong Kong. She was just a girl. In Hong Kong, the Chinese people live in huts on hillsides. I know. I saw it for myself in pictures."

What pictures had he seen, she wondered. She pictured the bustling, modern city she had visited just two years ago, when she first discovered her parents were alive there. But it struck her that he would not be interested in the truth. Finally, she asked, "How old was Philomena?"

"How old?" He looked at her as if the question were absurd. "How would I know?"

"Then what makes you think she was a girl?"

He finished off his coffee and stood up. "You do not believe me. But I tell you: this was true, this happened. I can't tell you how old she was, but she was a girl. Believe me, I know." With a flourish, he extracted a card from his wallet with his shop address, on which he wrote his home address and telephone.

"I invite you to my home," he said, handing her the card. "You can come with me right now if you like." He waited by the table.

Sai Yee looked at him, unable to respond.

And then, as abruptly as he had appeared, he walked away.

During her stay in Greece, Hui Sai Yee met many people who told her stories. Many of these she soon forgot. But Constantin's she remembered, although it was impossible to write anything about him. Once, she tried a portrait of a gambler, but found, after several drafts, that she had learnt nothing about gambling from him. The story of Philomena disturbed her, but she couldn't quite say why.

The day in January that her first novel was rejected she wandered around Upper Grosvenor Square, wondering how writers made a living if they didn't have other jobs or were independently wealthy. Grandma never complained, but Sai Yee didn't like asking for money from her to subsidize what little she could make doing pick-up work. UPI had already asked her to work for them in London. But writing a novel about her immigrant grandmother in Boston, was not linked, in her mind, to working for UPI.

It was then that she saw Constantin's portrait in the window of a gallery.

The Chinese artist stamp in the left corner read "Hui". Sai Yee asked the proprietor if by chance this was a Philomena Hui.

"Philomela Hui?" he repeated.

"No, Philomena," she said. "The saint, not the nightingale."

He smiled at her. Sai Yee could tell he liked the way she turned his slip of the tongue around. She thought he had a kind face. For the next fifteen minutes, he searched through papers on his desk and in his files, emerging at last with a triumphant "Aha, you're right."

Yes, he said, as he riffled through a file he'd found, her name was indeed Philomena with an "n", and she was from Hong Kong.

"Have you met her?" Sai Yee wanted to know. "I mean, how did you acquire this portrait?"

He frowned, trying to recall. "It must have been about a year ago, yes, that's right. She came in with some oils. Normally, I don't buy anything from someone who walks in off the street, but she seemed desperate for money. Some of her work was really quite good. On an impulse, I gave her a little something for a couple of the oils and this charcoal, which is the only piece I have left."

"What was she like?" And, to explain her curiosity, she added, "this may sound strange, but I think she might be a relative of mine whom I've never met. You see, we have the same surname, and I'm also from Hong Kong."

He was even more forthcoming after that. Yes, he remembered now, that she was a small woman, not particularly attractive, but rather able to command one's attention. Quiet though. Spoke as little as possible. How old? Oh, he couldn't say for sure but mid forties or fifty perhaps? A bit eccentric, but no more so than most artists. As an afterthought, he remarked that if she and Philomena were related, he couldn't see much family resemblance, and that of course the artist was much older than her.

Sai Yee bought the charcoal portrait — it startled her how exactly ugly Philomena had made him. She contemplated sending it to Constantin's shop. But, in the end, she kept the drawing. It was some time before she returned to Greece again, and when she did, Constantin had long been filed away as notes for a story that remained unwritten. The picture, however, she framed and hung over the bureau in her room in Grandma's Boston apartment, the one place she still called "home".

III

On the second morning of their honeymoon, Ralph Carder and Hui Sai Yee stood on a ledge of Hydra's coast, and stared at the large chest washed up by the Aegean onto the rocks below. It was fall. He climbed down to take a closer look. She followed.

"It's just like a Philomena Hui," said Sai Yee.

"You're right, you know," Ralph agreed. "But why?"

"Because you see it but can't see into it."

Ralph bent over the box and touched the damp, purplish tatters that covered it. Shreds of the rotted fabric came loose in his hand. He pushed it with his foot, but the box wouldn't budge.

"How long do you suppose it's been here?" she asked.

He knelt down and felt the base of the box. Sharp barnacles had formed which connected its base to the rocks. "Here, feel that," he said. "But watch your fingers."

She knelt close to him, and caressed the sharp roughness.

Ralph said, "It's sort of crusted, isn't it?"

Sai Yee pulled at the latch, but it wouldn't give. Rust flakes tinted her fingers a dirty orange.

"So what do you think of our treasure chest, darling?" He nestled his chin against her cheek.

"Is that what it is? Are you sure it isn't Pandora's box?"

He laughed. "Could be. Want to open it?"

She said, "Let's leave it alone."

He meant to say, I met Philomena once, you know, but didn't. At that same moment, she was thinking of Constantin, and wanted to tell Ralph that she felt a kinship with the mysterious Philomena, which was partly due to her supposed resemblance, but also didn't. A moment later, he was pushing her against the box in a playful tumble, and she, in answer, pulled his body tightly against hers, and they kissed, for awhile, on the rocks.

Later that day, they showered together. Sai Yee soaped the back of his neck, and he closed his eyes against the spray.

Only three months ago, this naked person behind him had bumped into him at an exhibit of Philomena Hui's "Stone Window And Other Works" on a London's summer evening, and had had the audacity to say, "Do you always meet women this way?" before introducing herself. And then to discover that she was from Boston, to which he was about to be transferred, and that she was planning to go home, and that she shared his love for Greece, and more importantly, Greek mythology, and. . . .

"We're on her island, you know," Sai Yee shouted over the jet of water. "Maybe we'll meet her."

Ralph stepped out of the shower and began drying himself. "I don't want to," he said.

"Why not?"

"We have better things to do on our honeymoon than track down iconoclastic painters from Hong Kong."

He regretted his lie immediately, and covered his face with the towel to avoid looking at her. He never wanted to see Philomena again! Often enough, he had wanted to tell Sai Yee about meeting Philomena. But he was too embarrassed by the whole incident. It made him look foolish.

The water gurgled down the drain in the shower as Sai Yee finished rinsing off. He felt her hand reach out from behind the curtain to rub his neck, and Philomena vanished from his thoughts.

At noon the next day, they sunbathed on a secluded rock plateau off the eastern coast of the island. Sai Yee watched Ralph dive into the Aegean. He was slender and graceful, like a seagull.

"The water's delicious," he shouted. "Join me?"

"Later. I want to read."

She watched Ralph swim away, disappearing behind a wall of rocks to the west. He had told her once that he could swim for hours.

For the next ten minutes, she tried to read, but her thoughts wandered to the new novel she had begun writing. An October honeymoon in Greece: what could be further away from life begun in China, and then with Grandma in Boston? Hadn't she told Ralph, when they first talked of marriage, that they were agreeably suited to each other because neither had relatives or friends to object? Ralph was an only child whose parents had both passed away. As for her, what did she really know about parents in Hong Kong whom she had separated from in China when she was eight? And her grandmother had passed away earlier this year, just after the Chinese New Year.

A twig snapped behind her.

She turned around. "Ralph?"

There was no reply.

"Is someone there?"

The silence frightened her. There was, as Grandma would say, a ghost.

"Tai dor gwai goo," she murmured. Too many ghost stories. Her momentary lapse into Cantonese startled her. She had a sudden remembrance of Constantin's face staring at her from the portrait in the London gallery.

Her imagination was over excited, she decided; she returned to her reading. A rustle of leaves sounded behind her. She turned quickly, and thought she saw a flag of long black hair disappear further up the slope, a breezy disturbance in its wake.

After they had made love, they lay together in the early morning hours. Sai Yee said, "Do you think Philomena has long hair?"

"Like yours, you mean?" he replied, stroking and coiling her thick strands.

She almost said, I'm told I look like her, but stopped herself. That presence, that "ghost" she had sensed earlier, had returned. She sat up.

"Darling, what's the matter?"

She did not reply, but got out of bed and proceeded to get dressed.

"What do you think you're doing, Sai Yee? It's four in the morning."

"Come on, let's go out."

"Where to?"

"The box by the sea. The one we found the other morning. You know, Pandora's."

He followed her, wondering, is my wife a little mad? As they headed towards the Aegean coast in the dark, he thought that Sai Yee did, in a way, remind him of Philomena.

Over her shoulder, Sai Yee said, "In Pandora's box, hope remained. The way the story goes, it isn't clear whether it was a barrel or a box. Nor is it clear who really opened the box, because in one version, it's Epimetheus her husband who opens it, although most accounts say Pandora opened it out of curiosity and accidentally unleashed evil in the world."

Ralph picked up her train. "Then there's the other Pandora story, of the original most beautiful woman created by Zeus as revenge upon mankind for the theft of fire by Prometheus. You know, woman as evil sent to destroy man, with or without the box. Sometimes, I think that version has more validity even though the other one's better known. Accidental curiosity seems too ungodlike an incident for the creation of evil."

They arrived at the box, and she felt the top.

"It's warm. Someone's been sitting on this," she declared.

"What on earth do you mean?"

"Philomena's been here."

He considered a moment. "Perhaps you're to write her story."

She embraced him, thinking that anyone else would have thought her mad. When he'd proposed, he said, "You won't have to work anymore for UPI. I'll support you. I want you to be free to write." How angry she had been at first! How they had fought as she tried to explain why she couldn't have some man support her. And he, uncomprehending, had said, "But don't you want to write?"

She stroked his hair, which was soft like a baby's. "You're probably right," she said, "perhaps I do have to write something about her." And then, feeling a wave of emotion overcome her, she exclaimed, "You're my benefactor. You want to save my artistic life, and I love you for it."

Her words held an uncomfortable ring for him, but he smiled and said, "Yes, you're right."

"When we get back to London, I'll quit my job. I won't work for them in Boston."

"All right," he said. And then, "I do love you, you know."

They left Hydra the next day.

"Let's go inland," she suggested. "Perhaps to Thessaloniki."

"Let's," he agreed.

They watched the port disappear as they sailed off. A pretty island, Ralph thought, but not terribly real. No cars allowed. A historically preserved sanctuary for visiting tourists to enthuse over. Overpriced rooms. Somewhere in the hills of Hydra, Philomena painted pictures that London's art-buying public celebrated.

Sai Yee said, "You know, I lived in Hong Kong for a short while with an aunt before I went to America. She lived in a building along this big waterfront road in Kowloon. I could look across the harbor and see the hills of Hong Kong Island. There are buildings dotted all over the hills there, just like here."

"And that's why she paints here. Is that what you mean?"

"I don't know."

They remained on deck in silence. It was a clear, crisp autumn morning. How complicated it was, thought Ralph, this whole business of knowing another person. Sai Yee smiled at him, and he wondered whether or not she read his thoughts.

"Do you suppose her stone window is on Hydra?" she asked.

"No." He had answered too quickly, he realized, seeing Sai Yee's puzzled look.

"How do you know?"

"She painted it before she moved here. Remember? It was in the notes for the exhibit."

"Was it?" She smiled.

They kissed. The boat chugged its way back to Athens. They passed the eastern coast of the island where Aegean waves broke against a crusted old box on the rocks. Had the lovers looked up, they might have caught a last glimpse of it. But they were too engrossed in their embrace to notice.

IV

At dusk, the man on Hydra known only as "Roach" sat at the waterfront cafe table farthest away from the pier. Ralph sat with him.

Roach scratched his pockmarked cheek, lit his pipe, spat, and took a sip of coffee. After a pause, he began speaking, beginning his story as he always did at any point that suited him at the time of telling. His English was good. People said he used to live in Athens years ago and learned his English from tourists.

"She used to recite a poem by Li Po, the famous Chinese poet" he began, "to maintain her *wa,* she said. *Wa* means harmony. It was important to her. She told me this translation of the poem:

> "*From bedside moon is bright,*
> *Lights up ground below.*
> *Raises head to see moonglow,*
> *Lowers head to recall village.*

"She could not recall, she said, her village. Then she would cry and cry, as if to remember were the most important thing. I told her to forget.

"Sometimes, she tried to paint. But she couldn't any longer; her hands shook too much."

"Was she alcoholic?" Ralph asked.

Roach waved his hand in a gesture of dismissal. "No, no, you don't understand. I'm a simple man. I can't explain these things well. But she wasn't an alcoholic. She was frightened, like a little girl.

"There was a man, Demetrius. He was young and tall, and very handsome, not ugly and fat like me. He loved her, and wanted her to marry him and take him to China. But he was a bad man, very lazy and shiftless. He preyed on women who visit our island, and made love to them. She despised him, but kept him around her.

"You see, I tell you she was lonely. She wanted this man to take care of her, but he couldn't. In the end, Demetrius went away one summer to Hollywood with an American woman who was very fat, but very rich. She was a hairdresser for the movie stars. She came to the port to see them sail away. Her eyes were angry and jealous. I watched her that day; I'd always watched her, even in the days when she still painted and was friendly towards foreigners. I knew that one day she would need me."

Roach coughed, and stopped to refill his pipe. He was thin and bony, and his gnarled hands were brown as the wings of a roach. It was hard for him to talk about her now that she was gone. And the cancer in his throat caused him pain. But he did talk, each week as he waited for her boat from Athens, to anyone who would listen. Now, he had been waiting for years.

"She had bad parents," he began suddenly. "They gambled. Her mother never suckled her, never taught her to be a woman. This was why she seemed to be a bad woman even though she wasn't."

"Why do you say she was 'bad'?" Ralph interrupted.

"Why do you need to ask? It is not I who call her bad, but people did. Because she gambles."

"In Athens? What does she play?"

"No, no." Roach gestured impatiently. "I only said she gambles. It is what she does with her life. I'm not talking about playing for money." He paused, and tapped his pipe which had gone out.

"Please," he continued, "let me go on and you listen. One night, after her screams, she told me about her life. I must tell you about the screams. Many, many months passed before I could get her to stop. I was tired, always looking after her. I caught very few fish during that time.

"It was about four or four thirty one morning. I was walking along the path to Kamini, where the road is high above the water. I heard her screams. It was a series of screams, unending. At first, I couldn't see where she was. All I knew was that those screams came from below, from near the sea.

"I began to climb down the rocks towards the source of the sound. When I found her, she was sitting like a bird on a big old box with her hands between her thighs. Just screaming."

"Like a nightingale," Ralph interrupted. "Or a swallow." He gazed into the distance with a faraway look in his eyes. "The daughters of the king of Athens."

Roach gestured impatiently. "You mix up my story. She wouldn't like that. Listen," he waved his hand at the audience, "she looked like a bird. That's all you need to know. So I continue.

"'Chinese woman,' I said to her, 'stop screaming.'

"She did not stop. It was as if she had not heard me. I said again, louder this time, 'Chinese woman, you must stop screaming.' But she carried right on.

"I was afraid that people would wake up and bring the police. I knew she must be ill — she had not been to the port for weeks. Perhaps, I thought, she had a fever. So I picked her up and threw her into the sea.

"Well, the screaming stopped at last, and I waited a few minutes to see if she could swim. When she looked like she was drowning, I jumped in and pulled her back to the rocks."

He stopped, and a satisfied smile appeared. His coarse, reddened, contorted features did not improve with his smile. He removed his cap, and scratched his slick, black hair.

"I took her to her home, undressed her, and put her to bed like a baby. She looked at me as if she did not know me, but I'm sure she recognized me. I've known her for a long, long time, but she was famous and I was not. I sat by her bed, and watched her sleep. From that night on, I began to live with her.

"After that, I would try to follow her to the rocks. She rarely spoke to me, hardly acknowledged my presence. She was very sly. When she wanted to scream she would sneak out without my knowing, and I would find her, perched like a bird on the box, screaming.

"Some mornings, she would mumble to herself in Chinese. It was important to her to remember her past. After all, she was not young even though she looked like a girl. When she noticed me, she would say, in Greek, 'Ghosts, ghosts. I won't let them have me. I will paint the insides of my mind.' You know, she speaks Greek beautifully. She even knows classical Greek. I wanted to get her off the rocks to hear her speak. On those mornings by the sea, she was bewitched by the Aegean and the dawn. She had no place for me."

Roach belched, and took another sip of coffee. Ralph stayed, and ordered Roach an ouzo. He gulped it down, and the waiter brought him a second glass which he held but did not drink.

A boat sailed into the harbor, and Roach stood up, squinted against the setting sun, his hand shading his eyes. As the boat neared, he sat down again.

"She's not coming back today," he declared, and gulped down the second ouzo. He relit his pipe, got up, and walked away.

Ralph sat until the sky was dark. His head hurt. The pain was getting worse. How long had he been coming here, to this island, in his search for the woman he loved? He used to know, used to count off each year he missed her. Now, he no longer counted.

Philomela and Procne, daughters of Pandion, king of Athens. Tereus violated them both, marrying Procne and imprisoning Philomela after severing her tongue, all without Procne's knowledge.

He began walking towards Kamini, towards his room. It was spring. Boston's spring air was bracing. The breeze was gentler here. And the island was covered with poppies and daffodils. Ralph climbed up a ridge overlooking the sea and stopped to watch the waves. Almost Easter. Almost time to crack blood red eggs at midnight after a feast of roasted lamb.

Procne got her revenge. She sacrificed her son, Tereus' child, and served his flesh to Tereus.

Ralph gazed at the sea for an hour, maybe longer. Sometimes, the sound of the waves eased the pain. At other times, the incessant pounding of the water frightened him, and he would run back to the hills, away from the shores. At Faneuil Hall one day, Sai Yee had said something like that. Or perhaps it was the day they walked around Chinatown and she saw her grandma's ghost. He couldn't remember.

Did Tereus enjoy the feast of his child Itys?

He continued along the path towards Kamini, his eyes trained on the rocks below. He hadn't seen the box, it seemed, for quite awhile. It was there somewhere. He knew it. Sai Yee had wanted to bring what she called the Philomena Hui box back to Boston. Ralph stopped in his tracks, startled by the clarity of this memory. There were moments he could remember exactly, the way things used to be, the way he once was. But the moments would pass, and he would lapse into an easy forgetfulness, recalling only an image of her.

Of who? Procne became a swallow and Philomela the nightingale. That's what the English poets say. Originally, it was the other way around because Philomela became the swallow that twitters but can't sing. Nightingales sing. They need their tongues.

The box was rusted shut. Ralph stopped searching the rocks and continued walking, his eyes on the path ahead. Philomena's body was small, like a girl's, the night they made love. It had to have been Philomena that night. He couldn't remember another woman there at the party who was as small. But he wasn't sure, couldn't ever be sure.

His head hurt.

Ralph climbed the stairs to his room on the second floor. He opened the unlocked door. Cooking smells emanated from his landlady's home below. She welcomed him back to Hydra each spring when he returned, and asked if he had enjoyed his autumn in Kea. It had been easy at the beginning. This year though, she seemed uneasy, almost a little unwilling to take him back. In the end, everything worked out fine. He paid her extra and explained his weight loss on his illness. His appearance had frightened her, he knew.

Philomela wove a tapestry depicting the story of her imprisonment and sent it to Procne. Sisters find a way to talk, even without a tongue.

Opposite his bed hung the Philomena Hui watercolor. A few years back, he had it verified as one of hers. It was valuable, one of the few known watercolors in existence. Ralph kept it on Hydra. When he was away, his landlady stored it for him.

He poured himself an ouzo and added water.

When Sai Yee had disappeared, suddenly one night . . . the pain became unbearable. Ralph lay down in bed, hoping it would go away. Memory increased the pain. He had to stop remembering, had to rid himself completely of the past. Only then would the agony end.

He stared at the picture. Chinese faces on buildings. The skyline of Hong Kong, of Philomena's village. The scarlet and gray swath of color captured him long before the buildings and faces. Sai Yee asked, the first time she saw it, is that perhaps her face on the center building, it's the only woman . . . what else had Sai Yee said? Ralph thought his head would burst.

Something someone said — it was the buildings, that drove her out, and the hordes of people, increasing all the time. Yet, in the stillness of Hydra, she claimed to find no peace. No Chinese in Greece, she said, except lonely cooks in Chinese restaurants. Who said? Philomena? Sai Yee?

Where was she now?

He watched the picture change in hue from scarlet and gray to blue and green. It changed quickly today, like an automatic remote flicking between television channels. Soon, the moving colors would settle into a mixture of oils thick on the canvas. Like a stone window.

Eventually, he knew, sleep would come. He waited for that moment, the time when all the voices could be stilled, except for her tongue-less murmurings, soothing his body to slumber.

Valediction

So let us melt, and make no noise
No tear-floods, nor sigh-tempests move,
'Twere profanation of our joys
To tell the laity our love.

— John Donne

London, 1989. Winter. Note in my *ga je*'s hotel room.

Dear muihmui,
Until we meet again.
Love.

Hong Kong, 1995. Fall. My fortieth birthday. Letter to my elder sister.

Dear *ga je*,

Do you remember that day, twenty or so years ago, in your *appartement* in Rouen, that modern if sterile place in a tower in the town you were going to leave once your husband got a job back in Paris . . . do you remember how you designed my sanctuary, the one I would some day have as a published, income earning novelist (yes I can hear you breathing an enormous sigh of relief — at last, about time)? You sketched every room for me — the monk's cell for my rough wooden writing desk; a cushioned reading space where the dumbwaiter led "downstairs" to an invisible kitchen and a cook who would cater to my every appetite; the library filled with shelves of books . . . and you promised you would one day commission an architect to build what you had drawn. When I saw Elvis' Graceland two years ago, and all those special rooms he designed, I remembered. But I don't want a Graceland; the imagined sanctuary of your charcoal sketches is all I need to survive my writing life.

And now, after the years have disappeared, vanished with my *gwailo* foreign devil husbands and insignificant others who no longer employ my life (thank god for US laws and alimony, however meager and late the payments), I finally found that space, albeit smaller and less grand than you originally imagined, and not a stone house in some coastal town along the eastern seaboard of the United States as you promised. It's taken me, oh a lifetime, or at least a few decades, moving and looking and striking out on new paths with such regularity that I am no longer surprising to any member of our internationally over-extended *wah kiu* family. When my first novel appeared in 1990, the Vancouver branch disowned me, you know, so there goes the last of the inheritance aspiration; the Singapore-singers-of-karaoke cousins refuse to keep my books at home as they consider them poison to the minds of their children; the clan in Java, that fried-in-peanut-oil-seriously-overcholesteralized horde of doctors, lawyers and pussy-whipped chiefs have told me I will never have the services of any of their chauffeured vehicles ever again (twice I was driven from Jakarta to Bandung and back to visit grandma's grave — for this I should be prostrate with gratitude); and the ones in Hong Kong are hugely thankful I write under a name that cannot be linked to theirs, since they must suffer me here in their city.

But what would amuse you most is our grandfather's reaction, issued edict-like from his haven in Perth. He said that what literary talents I had came from his branch of the family, but that it was a shame I chose to prostitute my talents in novels with "too much sex" instead of marrying a nice Chinese man (meaning Jen-Wei, his partner's grandson, who has more mistresses than condoms, but will inherit the fortune his father has amassed) the way he always told me I ought to, which would then free me to write about his life and the heritage of our family, a much "nobler" subject. Shades of *Red Chamber* nightmares! I must descend from a different lineage.

Dear *ga je* — Just what is family anyway? Bloodlines tie us. For me, marriage and relationships created even more "families" which I couldn't avoid or disavow, unless, like *Mission Impossible,* a disintegrating tape could disavow all knowledge once each episodic week — how I used to love that show; how you used to tease me about it.

Family aside, it's also this "overseas Chinese" *wah kiu* business that gets in the way. Grandpop never fails to remind us of our heritage as he updates the genealogical chart each year for the family and all its branches. (His latest thing, you know, is proving the purity of our Chinese blood, despite the Indonesian, Caucasian and even Latino bloods that have seeped their infectious way into the generations).

What kind of *dongxi* are we? How English fails me, despite all my English language novels! And *ga je,* how the Western world fails us for our most intimate expressions, our sense of family, our understanding of love.

Yet *c'est la vie,* isn't it, for this daughter of Hui.

Ga je, you'd probably like this flat I found back home in Hong Kong. Even by Paris standards, it's very large, over 1,500 square feet — 150 square meters to you. (I remember how you taught me that conversion. Helpful, as your teachings always turn out to be, because Hong Kong will be going more than merely metric in 1997.) But large it is, larger than your Paris apartment and a lot more expensive, though not a walk up of six flights (how did you endure it with baby Jean-Pierre on your hip, the shopping in your bag, and your briefcase of work . . . I always admired your energy, your stamina to get a PhD and married both in the same year, while I struggled to finish my bachelor's over six years, and then still didn't, during which you kept me going by the example of your life) — so my flat is enormous compared to our old home, and, well, luxurious. Yes, I hear you chiding me — *Muihmui!* Ever my spoilt girl.

But *ga je,* she's happy. You don't have to come and save her here.

Actually, you'd like it. It's in Mid-Levels, "miles away" from home in Hillwood Road. How faraway it seems to *ma mi* and *da di,* way across the harbor, even though it's only fifteen minutes from where they are in Tsimshatsui to Central by the MTR. You know, there's an escalator now that snakes from Central up to Mid-Levels, which stops at several roads. The Hakka women coolies of our girlhood would have appreciated this moving staircase cut into the hillside, even if it does go against the grain of the dragon. In fact, some evenings I almost see one of them around Staunton Street standing still on an escalator step, rising to the heavens, and dropping, for just a moment, the load of bricks balanced on two bamboo baskets hanging from a pole across her shoulder.

But the parents! We were always too "faraway" for them, weren't we? Sometimes, I think of them as frozen into a past tense of safety. The first time, at college, was at least invisibly faraway. I almost made it you know. The blood from my wrists was difficult to stanch, the nurse told you. But what I want to say is that I remember how you came to me when I called in the middle of the night, the night he asked you to marry him. Eight or nine hours on a Greyhound it must have taken from New York to my petty little Boston college world. How I must have terrified you. And perhaps, if I'd made it, you could have had a life.

This flat though. It's in an old, pre-war building, just like home. I bought some high wooden screens to separate the living and dining room, like the kind in Uncle Bian Lee's place in Mongkok, the ones in pawn shops *ma mi* used to take us to when she didn't want to show her face anymore at Uncle's place, entreating him for yet another loan, pretending she was pawning her family's jewelry because she didn't care for it. The ceilings are, oh, twelve feet I'd say. Two lengths of my current lover would almost fit to the top — no, I know you don't want to hear about yet another one so I'll spare you the details, but at least he isn't a husband, no, don't roll your eyes at me — he's a Northern Chinese dissident poet from Beijing, they're the best kind, dissidents, that is.

But you! Living your almost perfect life. Married to an almost acceptable husband. You're the only woman I know of in this day and age who married the man who took her virginity — even Hong Kong women don't do that anymore. Even though he was French-American, at least he spoke beautiful Mandarin. *Da di* never had the grace to compliment him, but at least you could see how pleased he was to be able to converse in Mandarin with his son-in-law, after years of suffering the indignity of Hong Kong's Cantonese-speaking populace who made fun of his accent. Yes, he was hopeless, wasn't he! And still is, despite all his years of Chinese school in Indonesia and his fluent Mandarin. But he gets his own back. A Cantonese trying to speak Mandarin is worse than an Australian speaking English — that's what he still says.

Valediction

There's a tree outside my flat. A sprawling banyan. A pair of white cockatoos and a squirrel live in it. It reminds me of the tree we used to climb in the park near our school, the one out of which I fell and suffered a huge bruise on my forehead. You took care of me, took me to the hospital, and then rang the parents to summon them to fetch us because you didn't have enough money for a taxi. How old were you then? Only twelve at most I think.

But those cockatoos. They're not supposed to be there. Escaped from the Botanical Gardens, I think, or some such story. Who knows? All I'm certain of is that they shouldn't be in my banyan tree, no more than I should be in this city, this supposed home city of ours. I'm not like the squirrel; he belongs. He's got the right reflexes.

But here I am. It's a third-floor flat, an easy walk up. The parents haven't seen it yet, haven't displayed even the slightest curiosity, but then again you know how they are. They never visited my other place either, the one which my news-anchor lover rented when I lived here previously, and that was in Kowloon, albeit "miles" away on Broadcast Drive.... Why am I complaining? Because they made it to your wedding halfway round the world, and gave you a dowry of jewelry and money fit for the queen that you are?

Why am I so sure you'd like my sanctuary?

When we were young, do you remember how I hated the sea, because, I said, going in was always like taking a lukewarm bath. You were the queen who called me princess, and told me stories about my special *petit prince* on a flying black horse who would steal me away to another planet. Our new world had fields of poppies and daffodils, lots of them all over the hillsides, surrounded by an ocean of icy-cold water into which I could dive and swim for miles. And it was quiet; there were no cars.

Remember the second time you rescued me? I had plunged into the Charles River in winter, and the nurses were trying to thaw me out. When you arrived by plane from New York, I was still hallucinating from the mushrooms and babbling about planetary horses. The nurse's aide said to you that I thought I was *le petit prince,* to which you replied, I was. How we laughed over that afterwards when you held me and welcomed me back! And I begged you not to tell our parents and you promised me you wouldn't. You kept that promise, too, didn't you?

Ga je! How did you love me so long?

Did I remember to say I moved into this flat in summer, at the beginning of summer? I missed the rains the day the movers arrived with all my things from New York. The very next day, it poured. Nothing's worse than wet boxes brought into an old flat where damp rises, the way it does here. The ceiling in my study is streaking through the new coat of paint. The landlord did paint, and cleaned after a fashion. But he's off in Canada somewhere, and leaves these details to his sister who manages his property. No children. He refused to rent to anyone with children. The flat stood empty for awhile. A three-bedroom 1,500 square foot flat simply doesn't get snapped up by couples with no children. It is a flat for a Hong Kong family.

You would know how to make a home of it, with your children and your Shanghainese man.

Don't you understand how much *da di* and *ma mi* would have liked him? Oh I know he spoke accented Mandarin, which *da di* would have commented on, but at least his English was good enough for *ma mi.* And you and he could have jabbered with the children in French. Funny but for all your intelligence, without a doubt superior to mine, you just never understood about blood-lines. All you had to do was leave that husband, show up with your man and children in tow on the parental doorstep, and they would never have turned you away.

You don't believe me? No, I guess you would have a hard time believing me, divorced twice over the way I was, having affairs with local Hong Kong painters who exhibited my naked body across canvases in Hong Kong's art galleries with a clear representation of my face — poor *ma mi,* she couldn't face any of her friends for weeks when that happened. But I did it all here, not "faraway" in New York. It was we who were far, not they. Homage is paid to the Middle Kingdom — that is, to every Chinese parent that ever existed — not the other way around. I know each of my many returns was fraught with scandal, or the possibility of yet another familial loss of face. But I came home, like a dutiful daughter, for *ma mi* to weep over in shame. I didn't deny her that pleasure.

When Amelia was born, the parents diligently studied the photos you sent. How fortunate she came after Jean-Pierre. Don't you remember how all your baby things were embroidered with W for William, since they were convinced of your masculinity? *Ah non!* you say, our parents were not that Chinese, being as they were *wah kiu,* and never threading into Hong Kong society completely. Why do you think they waited so long before having me? Not to risk another disappointment? Or was I an accident? They'll never say, and we'll never know. So it's the guessing game, the favorite pastime of Chinese life.

But when Amelia was born . . . they studied those photos for a long time. Finally, *da di* looked up at both *ma mi* and me and declared, "She looks Chinese, thank goodness."

It was just before I took the trip to New York and OD'd on speed and Jim Beam. Remember that trip? That was my watershed attempt; you began your talking cure with me after that, once a week at great telephone expense to yourself and your family. And you stayed with me, sometimes for weeks at a time, or had me stay with you. Do you wonder that my brother-in-law found himself a few girlfriends?

Stoic sister, you should be in this flat of mine with your wonderful Shanghainese man. He truly loved you, perhaps even more than your husband did. The only reason I can afford it is because I'm the "right profile". The landlord said he would rent it to me because his sister was my schoolmate and vouched for me, actually told him he had enough money and should see his way clear to supporting a penniless writer who was after all, "one of us". So yes, I live in luxury for a song because the schoolmate was once my lover and this way she knows there's less chance (though not no chance) that I'll keep our affair out of my novels and away from her very wealthy and socially prominent husband's eyes. I'm not immune to bribery.

You haven't always liked my "right" profile, have you? I can't say I blame you. Being right, the way it worked for me, was about being wrong, but taking that wrongness to such extremes (call it selfishness, license, self-indulgence — whatever it was, it worked, and, unlike Miller, I didn't even have to prostitute my lover for my daily bread) that it became the only way to be, the way everyone expected me to be. It was my *libération,* my *jie fang.* I didn't always like your responsible nature, your willingness to accept the roles dished out by Confucius and other tyrants. The charm of my irrepressible irresponsibility, backed by just enough talent, squeaked me by, especially in our shallow city where a little melodrama goes a long way for lack of anything deeper to observe. Besides, I was good gossip for the party circuit. You chastised me, scolded me mercilessly as all good *ga je*s are supposed to do. But you never blamed my writing, the way the family did, because they couldn't understand, could they, why I had to do what I did instead of getting a job or married properly, the way I was supposed to.

I know now I was born to write. In your own way, you tried to tell me, without placing the pressure of being accepted on me, without expectation of livelihood or success (how I've appreciated your many bailout loans for my extravagances over the years), without condemning the myriad wrong turns I took in pursuit of what I thought the artistic life should be. You painted my real dream, made me think, despite all proof to the contrary, that it was possible. Things only came true if you said they would. I am about so much fiction and always have been. You are about fact, about facing life the way it is, the way it has to be.

So why has this farewell taken so long to say, since that departure on your fortieth birthday?

You told me once you would not live past forty. It was in Paris, at the worst point of your marriage. I was young and "recuperating" from my most recent attempt. Have you forgiven me for not really knowing what you meant? Oh what am I saying? Of course you've forgiven me. You've always forgiven me.

But I should have known what you meant!

I think I understand. We were close in time and space. You changed my diapers; we fought on our parents' bed. I went after you with a knife and fork once when we were little, angry over some imagined hurt. So how could I not understand?

If nothing else, we could have lived in this flat together with your children. It's big and beautiful and spacious. I don't have the married lover anymore. He comes to Hong Kong often, which is ironic because, now that I've moved here where it would be much easier to see him because he travels out this way all the time, I've dumped him back in New York along with the husband. You know, the one you never thought much of, but didn't have the heart to say so? I know. You were right. You looked upon my husbands and lovers with disdain, and rightly so. Men let you down, you always said.

So why did you believe in love and romance and promises of forever? (You were dreadful that way — despite my multiple lovers I didn't really fall in love the way you did.) I think it helped you survive adolescence, and, for a time in Paris, your marriage. And then your Shanghainese came along. A Chinese doctor! And the son of a respectable businessman. What a perfect *wah kiu* son-in-law he would have made for the parents. He even wanted to come live in Hong Kong. You should at least have had an affair with him. But no, it was only love you wanted, and love you got. He called me once, to see if I could convince you to leave your husband. You wouldn't listen. And in the end he married, and that was the end of your second chance at love and happiness.

Of course your husband shouldn't have left you, despite the fact that we all knew it wasn't a marriage worth saving by then. Of course you shouldn't have disappeared to England that day the way you did, so that he could complain about how you just "upped and left your children" (what a hypocrite, he left you after all, and it's not like Amelia and Jean-Pierre were left alone for any length of time since your mother-in-law was coming to visit that evening).

But it's too many years now to blame my brother-in-law any longer. He could also be forgiven for his flings with mistresses. After all, you were busy with the children, and me. Even I couldn't expect him to understand your devotion to such a prodigal, profligate and ungrateful sister. You never even told him about your own love affair, such as it was. What absolute fidelity your marriage inspired in you! As long as you could be in love, and if not that, as long as the marriage held, you could remain with me, with all of us.

Your children do remarkably well you know — I've been going to see them at least twice a year, and they still ask me to tell them stories every time. So I tell them about all the worlds beyond their own. It's the least I can do for my family.

You gave up on romance, didn't you? Perhaps if you had held onto the magic of falling in love ... but for what happened in London afterwards I blame myself — for not coming when you called, for not being there the one time you asked for help. Which is why I am no longer married to the man who stopped me, who whined his jealousy, even though you had never, in all those years, ever asked for a favor. Why didn't you shout? Why didn't you scream? Why didn't you din into my stupid head the real reason for your call, instead of coating your pain, the way you always do, because who I was, what I was, had to dominate the space between us? In the end, even that husband of mine wasn't to blame — he always whined.

Who wasn't he, the man who killed you? Why wasn't he there for you to fall in love with, to become starry-eyed over, like in all those romance novels you loved to read as a girl? Why didn't he materialize just one more time, to offer a bit of hope for surviving your divorce, your life?

Just like all your romance novelists, I let you down, didn't I? Me and the man who wasn't. And the husband who no longer could be.

What triggered it that day? Why that day? I've turned it over and over again in my mind, to no answer, no lightening of the mystery. But it's not a mystery, is it? I can almost hear what you'd say —

Death needs no pride, no *raison d'être*. It's life that demands our devotion and love.

I only know how to write my kind of novels now. Writing's the one promise I made to anyone that I've kept and will keep — when you told me that last time on the phone to write, always write no matter what, how could I know that my promise was what you needed to hear, to know you'd completed the last of your family obligations? I imagine you calling, first our parents, then your ex, then your children. Finally your *muihmui*. "Little sister," how softly you said it. Even when you asked me to come, it was less a plea than a request, understated, the way you always are in life, and in death.

You didn't even leave a mess. How like you to be so neat, to leave no blood, to have slept into your overdose in the bathtub so that cleaning up would be no problem. Just a body in a hotel room, with the exact cash payment on the dresser next to the hotel bill you had asked for the night before. And my phone number on the envelope of that three-line note.

I keep it, along with your sketches of my sanctuary.

Dear ga je.
Until we meet.
All my love.
Muihmui.

About the Author

Born and raised in Hong Kong by Chinese-Indonesian immigrant parents who "spoke too many languages", Xu Xi (Sussy Chakó) has been writing and publishing fiction since the age of eleven. She lived and traveled in Asia, Europe and America. After eleven years on the US East Coast, she returned to Asia. She now lives in Hong Kong and works for an international advertising agency.

Her first novel, *Chinese Walls*, was published by Asia 2000 in 1994. Other fiction has appeared in various magazines, literary periodicals and anthologies, including — *Manoa, Home To Stay: Asian American Women's Fiction* (published by Greenfield Press), *The Hawaii Review, Short Story International, Phoebe, Lovers* (a Crossings Press anthology), *Hawaii Pacific Review,* among others, and her work has also been broadcast on the BBC's World Service. She was awarded a 1991 New York State Arts Foundation fiction fellowship, and was the 1992 *South China Morning Post* short story contest winner. Some of her earlier works were published under her Indonesian name Sussy Komala. She also writes occasional articles for magazines and newspapers in Asia.

By the same author, (writing as Sussy Chakó)

Chinese Walls

"Although simply written, *Chinese Walls* tells a complex and controversial story of a Chinese family. The author goes boldly where other, perhaps overly-sensitive, Asian authors fear to tread in tackling such subjects as sex, Aids, homosexuality, incest and adultery.

"The story concerns an overseas Chinese family living in Hong Kong from the 1960s to the 1990s. Narrated by Ai-lin, the family's youngest child, *Chinese Walls* wraps in vivid colour the dramatic changes that have taken place during three decades in the territory.

"Vividly, she describes the mother forcing the children into reciting Chinese dynasties in Mandarin, the little girl's curiosity about the prostitutes in Chungking Mansions and the night of incest between sister and brother — her only happy memory of family life."

— **Angelica Cheung,** *Eastern Express*

Other titles
from
Asia 2000

Non-fiction

Burman in the Back Row	*Aye Saung*
Burma's Golden Triangle	*André and Louis Boucaud*
Cantonese Culture	*Shirley Ingram & Rebecca Ng*
Concise World Atlas	*Maps International*
Foreign Investment & Trade Law in Vietnam	*Laurence Brahm*
Getting Along With the Chinese	*Fred Schneiter*
Hong Kong Pathfinder	*Martin Williams*
Korean Dynasty — Hyundai and Chung Ju Yung	*Donald Kirk*
Walking to the Mountain	*Wendy Teasdill*

Fiction

Chinese Walls	*Sussy Chakó*
Cheung Chau Dog Fanciers' Society	*Alan B Pierce*

Photo Books

Bayan Ko! — Images of the Philippine Revolt	*Project 28 Days*
Beijing Spring	*Peter and David Turnley*
Beyond the Killing Fields	*Kari René Hall*
USSR: The Collapse of an Empire	*Liu Heung Shing*

Order from Asia 2000 Ltd
1101 Seabird House, 22–28 Wyndham St
Central, Hong Kong
tel (852) 2530 1409; fax (852) 2526 1107
URL: http://www.asia2000.com.hk